captain dead man

Sweetfern Harbor Mystery - 3

wendy meadows

Majestic Owl Publishing LLC
P.O. Box 997
Newport, NH 03773

❀ Created with Vellum

chapter one

Brenda Sheffield twirled her hand around to focus on every aspect of the beauty of the ring Mac Rivers had just slid onto her finger. The sun glistened on the intricate facets of the diamond in its delicately pronged setting. Her eyes matched the sparkling stone when she looked up into his eyes.

"I love you, Mac Rivers. I want to be with you forever."

"I will love you forever, too, my love." He looked into her eyes as if he could see forever written there.

She leaned her head closer to the man she loved, her heart beating joyfully in her chest. Brenda wanted the magic spell of this moment to last the rest of her life, but she stepped back when she heard voices from a distance.

"Here come Allie and Phyllis," said Mac with a half-smile.

Brenda turned to look with a huge grin on her face. "I can't wait to tell them the news."

She watched the two women cross the sprawling lawn behind the Sheffield Bed and Breakfast where Mac had just asked her to marry him.

Mac looked at the two employees of the bed and breakfast, and back at the owner, his new fiancé.

"Wait a while before we announce it," he said. He smiled

at her baffled look. "There will be plenty of time to spread the news. Right now, you will be busy with the upcoming boat race and I'm sure your bed and breakfast will be sold out of rooms. That alone will keep you seriously occupied." He didn't like the cloud that crossed her face and tried to amend his words. "Let's just wait until everything settles down again and then we can talk about whether to shout it from the rooftops."

Brenda's face fell for a moment before she took a breath and then finally answered. "If you think that's best, then I'll wait." As Allie and Phyllis approached, she didn't have time to consider his words and so simply tucked them in the back of her mind. She turned toward Allie Williams, her office assistant, and her housekeeper, Phyllis Lindsey. It would be very hard to keep this news from her employees at the Sheffield Bed and Breakfast. It would be especially hard to keep it from Phyllis, who had become her best friend and confidant. At the last moment, Brenda turned the ring over to hide the gem and clasped her right hand over her left one. She thought to herself that perhaps later she would ask Mac to take it back until he was ready for them to make the announcement to everyone – but why didn't he want her to tell everyone right away? Her disappointment turned to unhappiness, which she managed to squelch within her. He had his reasons and she would be patient, for now, but the issue would have to be discussed soon.

"Brenda, there is a young couple here with a baby. We wanted to ask if they could have the room in the back of the second floor," said Allie. "I know it means switching them with the older couple coming in, but with the baby…we thought its cries might disturb the other guests if they were in the front room."

Phyllis interjected. "Of course, we don't know if the baby will be a crier or not, but just in case, don't you think it would be better for them to be away from the others?"

Brenda felt relief spread through her. Switching back to what she knew best was comforting. "That's a good idea. The older couple won't arrive until closer to dinnertime. They've not been assigned a room at this point and they didn't give any instructions or preferences in regard to which room when they made their reservation, did they, Allie?"

"No, they didn't ask for anything special. I believe they are devoted hikers and the wife told me the stairs won't bother them. They're in their sixties, but she told me they have won commendations for some of their hiking expeditions."

They chatted a little longer about the guests who were expected to arrive and then as a group, headed back toward Sheffield House. As they reached the porch, before the women turned to go back inside, Phyllis looked at Brenda in a curious manner. Her housekeeper and good friend knew her better than anyone had ever known her. Brenda, who had kept unusually quiet, avoided the scrutiny of her gaze until Phyllis seemed to take the hint and finally decided to follow Allie back inside. When they were at last out of earshot, Brenda turned back to Mac.

"If I can't tell anyone our news yet, I think it would be better if you hold on to the ring until I can. There is no way I can wear it without questions," she said unhappily, twisting the ring around her finger again.

Mac was visibly taken aback. "Why not keep it in your apartment until after the boat races? Then we'll decide together when it is time." He bit his lip watching her look of unease, knowing he had cast a shadow over their moment of happiness, and he couldn't take it back.

Brenda's heart ached a little to look at the man she loved and to realize they had had a disagreement like this only moments after she had just felt such intense joy at his proposal. She wanted nothing more than to believe his words and wait until the hustle and bustle of the boat races was over to make the big announcement. But something made her hold back from asking him why, and that something made her heart ache all the harder.

Mac searched her face as if he wanted to lift her spirits with the sheer force of his smile. "You did a great job when the Seaside Theatre Festival was here, Brenda. Everyone in town was impressed by how smoothly the performances went. I know you had a lot to do with that by the way you answered every need the performers had while they stayed at the bed and breakfast."

"That's to say nothing of the horrible events everyone went through." Brenda was lost in thought for a moment, thinking back to the tragic murder of the star of the show, a well-known and admired actress. "I've had to go out of my way to make sure the bed and breakfast didn't get a bad reputation just because someone committed a hideous crime here. It was so awful, but it wasn't our fault."

"That murder is still the talk of the town. You were outstanding in getting to the right suspect, too. Again, I'm so very sorry I doubted your innocence in the matter." Brenda didn't respond. She felt it was all in the past and wished intensely that the subject hadn't come up right on the heels of their disagreement. She sensed that Mac knew it was time to change the subject again. He cleared his throat before continuing, "You know, I have a very good friend who is a fellow detective, from Brooklyn. His name is Bryce Jones. He grew up here in Sweetfern Harbor. He knows all about how you were the one who solved Ellen Teague's murder and he wants to meet you."

Brenda's eyes grew wide. "I didn't know word spread like that."

Mac laughed. "I can assure you everyone in my field knows you from coast to coast. Ellen Teague was a pretty famous name and you were bound to become famous yourself when you figured things out." He bent and kissed her. "I have work to do and so must move along. I love you, Brenda, and I'm more than happy you accepted my proposal." He clasped her hands gently in his own and then let go and walked off across the lawn, back to his car.

After he left, Brenda slipped the engagement ring off her finger and dropped it into the pocket of her slacks. With a kind of heaviness in her heart that she tried to ignore, she went to her apartment and secured the sparkling ring in a locked case. As she turned the key, she told herself firmly, the ring is as safe as his love for me. But she had a nagging feeling of sadness as she pushed the case to the back of the drawer.

Her thoughts moved to Bryce Jones. She was curious about him. It was the first time Mac had mentioned the name to her, though there had never been a reason to do so before now, she thought. Perhaps a visit from Mac's friend would be a welcome distraction during the busy week. After all, it might be nice to trade tips and tricks with an old pro who appreciated her skills.

She went back downstairs. On the wall along the staircase hung nautical paintings her uncle had procured for the Sheffield Bed and Breakfast before his death. When she walked into the dining room, one painting caught her eye. The sky in the painting was as blue as the ocean, only the texture of the surface changed between the two expanses of blue. It was so real she could almost guess where the artist had been sitting by the harbor when he had painted it. She knew the painting's subject told of a boat race twenty years ago. Every July the races were held in Sweetfern Harbor. In the blue distance of the ocean in the painting were the bright sails of three outstanding boats as they raced past under a brisk wind.

"I love that painting especially," said Phyllis. Brenda turned quickly to see her housekeeper standing a few feet from her. "Those boats have raced here every year. They've always had the same captains, though I think they've rebuilt or bought newer boats over the years." She pointed to each one as she named them. "That's the Scully and this one is the Pratt. The third one is called the Eddy. They are owned by three men who have been close friends and fierce competitors for several decades now."

"I guess it's a deeper tradition than I realized," said Brenda, examining the tiny boats in the distance of the painting.

Phyllis kept her eyes on the painting and nodded her head in agreement. "There is a $50,000 prize for the winner, but they look forward to winning the silver cup most of all." She smiled. "Of course, I'm sure the money is coveted, too, but they probably spend it all on fixing up their boats each year. That silver cup is the crown of the race."

They talked of the many events that would herald the annual race on the water until Phyllis excused herself, saying she had one more room to clean. The rest of the guests would be arriving soon.

As she turned to go up the stairs, Phyllis turned to Brenda and said, "Oh, and by the way...the last room just got booked. We'll have a detective visiting from Brooklyn. Maybe Mac has mentioned him to you? Mac is older than him, but they were next door neighbors and every kid on the block grew up playing together. He and Bryce Jones, along with Bryce's older brother, used to get into plenty of trouble when they were young." Phyllis was momentarily lost in memories of the past. "But I suppose Mac has told you all about Bryce."

"He just mentioned him to me a little while ago," Brenda said, but she didn't voice aloud the rest of her thoughts. She wondered why Mac failed to mention his friend would be her guest. She had not gone over the guest list with Allie yet, but it was next on her list. "What else do you know about him? Is he a good detective?"

"From what I've heard, he is good at his job." Phyllis

hesitated. "This is off topic, but I have a secret to tell you, Brenda. We don't want the word out yet, or at least Molly doesn't, but...she is engaged to be married! I can't believe my daughter will be a married woman within the year." Phyllis was beaming. "But please don't tell anyone. She's not quite ready to put the news out there. She says it's because every tidbit of news spreads too fast in this town. They want to keep it to themselves a while longer."

Her smile was wistful. Brenda understood instantly how anxious Phyllis must be to spread the news about Molly and Pete Graham, and how hard it was to wait. Brenda expressed her happiness at the news and simply bit her tongue about the rest. She wished so badly she could tell her friend her own news, but she held back as promised to Mac. She left Phyllis and headed for the office. She and Allie looked at the guest list. The young couple with the baby had settled in and were happy with their room. It was almost time for the rest to arrive for their stays. Both women looked up when they heard footsteps in the foyer.

Allie went out to the desk to greet the handsome man in front of her. "Hello, welcome to Sheffield Bed and Breakfast. Are you...um, that is, are you checking in?" Allie dimpled with her best smile at the new guest, whose good looks almost threatened to make her forget what she was doing.

"I'm Bryce Jones, and I have a reservation."

Brenda came out of the office and introduced herself. "Mac told me you are his friend, and a detective in Brooklyn. I understand you and Mac have known one another for many years." Brenda too couldn't take her eyes from the extremely good-looking man in front of her. Penetrating deep, his gray eyes focused on her. Fit, tanned, and very well-dressed, Bryce Jones looked much younger than either she or Mac. He flashed a quick smile at her and she blinked and looked down at some paperwork as she tried to get her wits about her. She surmised he was in his mid to late thirties.

7

But he wasn't deterred. He leaned in to the counter. "Ah, Brenda. At last I get to meet the famous amateur sleuth. Your reputation has spread far and wide. From what I've heard, perhaps you should drop the word 'amateur' from your resume." Brenda was surprised at his words even though Mac had said the same thing about her name getting out. His head tilted slightly to one side and the grin spread across his face. "I can't believe you outsmarted Detective Mac Rivers. I heard he tried to arrest you for some unfathomable reason. I mean, who could ever find it in his heart to arrest such a beautiful young woman?"

Allie exchanged a quick glance with Brenda and hid a smile. She noted a slight flush creeping into her boss's face.

"I have your registration all set," Allie cut in. She hoped to spare Brenda further embarrassment.

The sixteen-year-old found it hard to take her eyes from their guest. He smoothly took the key to his room from Allie while his eyes remained fixed on the owner of Sheffield Bed and Breakfast as she stammered a little, thanking him for his kind words. Brenda welcomed him again and told him if he needed anything, to ask any staff member. All heads turned when the door opened again. Mac Rivers looked at Brenda's flushed face and then greeted his friend with a firm slap on his shoulder. "I take it you're here for the boat races, Bryce."

"You know me too well. I haven't been back here for several years and yearned for my former home again. Plus, I couldn't hide my curiosity about Sweetfern Harbor's newest detective," he finished with a conspiratorial glance at Brenda.

Mac grinned at his friend's words and then spoke to Brenda. "I left my cell phone here a little while ago. I'll go outside and see if it's still on the table near where we were sitting."

"I have it right here. Phyllis just brought it in a short time ago. I was going to call the station and let you know," said

Allie helpfully, offering him the phone from where it had been sitting behind the desk.

Mac thanked her and took the phone. His eyes clouded when he turned to see Bryce, whose eyes seemed locked onto Brenda as he peppered her with short questions about the bed and breakfast. He hoped the man would enjoy the races and then leave for Brooklyn as soon as possible. He couldn't be trusted around women.

"Did Susan come with you?" Mac asked his friend deliberately, clamping one hand down on the younger man's shoulder.

"Who? Oh, Susan. We broke up last week. It was a good thing. She's a little too clingy and I had to let her go." He laughed easily and glanced at Brenda again. She was certain he winked at her and when she looked at Mac, she was sure he saw the same thing. She looked down and could suddenly feel herself blushing. Was this handsome young man flirting with her in front of Mac? Before she had time to answer that question, Mac swooped in and saved her.

"Brenda, I thought you'd like to meet the three famous captains in town," said Mac. "I just saw Molly Lindsey. She mentioned they were in her coffee shop. Do you have time to walk down there with me and meet them?"

Brenda was happy for the much-needed distraction. "I'd love to meet them. Phyllis was just telling me all about the famous racing families."

Mac reached for her hand and gently pulled her toward the door and out from beneath Bryce's clutches.

"Word is that the town is just packed with tourists again," Brenda added, trying gamely to speak politely to her guest and to Mac, who was obviously trying to get her to leave quickly.

"Yes, people come from far and wide for the sailing race. I know neither of us can spend a lot of time away from our work, so now may be the only chance to meet the three captains. They are experts in sailboat racing and come from old seafaring families," said Mac. "A lot of knowledge is stored in those three brains when it comes to living and working on the water. By now, they are all retired and spending their money and time on boats. There is a healthy competition between them." Mac finally succeeded in getting her out the door and away from Bryce's piercing gray eyes.

Bryce watched until they closed the door behind them. He shrugged his shoulders and told Allie he would get settled in.

"When you feel like it, we have refreshments in the sitting room," she said brightly. Allie gestured across the hallway to indicate the sitting room and secretly hoped their attractive guest would spend plenty of time mingling. Bryce thanked her and went upstairs to his room. Allie's eyes happily followed him until he turned toward his room at the top of the stairs.

chapter two

When Brenda and Mac walked into the busy coffee shop, there was one available table. Jovial voices drifted toward them and Mac led her to where the famous captains sat drinking their coffee. Brenda was at last introduced. The first man, Captain Scully, sported a bushy, white beard and looked like the epitome of the salty fisherman she was sure he was. Before she could turn to the other two men, Captain Scully took her hand and shook it vigorously.

"I could tell you some stories, young lady," he said. "Maybe we'll have time to do that when this race is over." He laughed in a deep-throated tone. "This man next to me is old Captain Pratt. He doesn't know it yet, but I'm going to beat him this year."

Captain Pratt was quick to retort. For a few minutes, he relayed a couple of incidents that caused Brenda to laugh in merriment and shudder in fright at his daring escapades in former races. It was obvious that Captain Pratt was not afraid to take risks or to do whatever it took to win any contest. His red hair was tinged with streaks of grey and he had fierce emerald eyes that sank deep beneath his brow, though they were still bright and merry. A lifetime of faint freckles covered his face and arms.

"And this man next to me is Captain Eddy. As you can tell by now, our boats all hold our own names. He's the owner of the Eddy just as I own the Pratt and Scully owns the Scully." He laughed good-naturedly.

Captain Eddy was the more reserved of the three. He shook Brenda's hand firmly but she felt that his grasp was gentle. He smiled at her and she sensed he was a man of few words compared to the other two. His strong physique told of living a life on the seas.

Once introductions were made, Captain Scully interrupted himself as he began to tell another uproarious story, saying "You must come tour our ships, Miss Brenda. If you are interested, there will be time for that before the races tomorrow."

"Now, now, Captain Scully, who are you dragooning onto your crew today?" A voice spoke up and they turned to the scraping of a chair. A man with thickly muscled forearms and a lean, muscled physique pulled the chair up next to the table and sat down.

"I'm Wally Doyle, shipwright and builder of boats since probably before you were born. I've wanted to meet Randolph Sheffield's niece ever since you came to Sweetfern Harbor. I was glad he left the bed and breakfast to you. We all miss Randolph."

Brenda thanked him and then asked, "Did you build all of their boats?"

"I sure did. These three are like brothers and so the boats they're racing this year are identical. They wanted matching boats to begin with, but I decided it would be a fairer race if none of these rascals could say one boat had some kind of advantage over the other, too. They can be such vicious competitors when it comes to these boat races. You've never seen such a pack of old biddies clucking over whose pie will win at the county fair as these three worrying over the silver cup!" He laughed at his joke and slapped Captain Eddy heartily on the back.

Captain Eddy shook his head and smiled. Pratt made a joke about making sure he would go over every inch of the vessel again to make sure Wally did a good job. Scully laughed loudly and stated he had no worries along those lines. The three of them started ribbing each other over the details of long ago races and they all laughed easily together. It was obvious to Brenda they enjoyed a deep comradeship between them. More tourists and locals entered the shop and it seemed like everyone wanted to stop by the table and say hello to the captains and wish them luck in the race. Brenda and Mac excused themselves and ordered coffees to go. As they went to leave Morning Sun Coffee, they stopped by to thank Scully for the invitation to tour the boat. The other two captains chimed in to welcome them onboard as well.

"They are quite a group," said Brenda as they stepped back out onto the sidewalk and into the fresh ocean breeze of Sweetfern Harbor. "I'm looking forward to touring their boats. I've never been on a racing sailboat."

Mac smiled, saying "Captain Scully invited you because they all believe that if a beautiful woman steps onto the deck of a boat it will bring the captain good luck."

Brenda laughed. "I didn't know that. Then I guess I'd better go onto all three of them to be fair." She was beginning to feel the excitement of the upcoming race. The town was alive with expectation. She overheard several conversations among the tourists and locals that they passed by, and it seemed like many were making bets on the winner.

It was a beautiful day for their walk, but when Brenda and Mac reached the bed and breakfast again, she saw that he had become pensive. She wondered what was on his mind and was ready to ask him when he spoke. His words were unexpected.

"Bryce Jones is a flirt. He's an old friend but he has a reputation. Don't let him get to you, Brenda. If you have any trouble with him, I want to know it. He won't hold back and is known to make some women uncomfortable with the way he comes across." He kissed her.

"Mac...you know you have nothing to worry about. I've seen how flirtatious your friend is, but he's nearly fifteen years younger than me! Surely he has many irons in the fire." Mac laughed at her joke, but she could see that he was still troubled.

She purposefully didn't mention the fact that Bryce wasn't hard on the eyes. She only had eyes for Mac, but somehow she doubted that Mac was in the mood to discuss Bryce's romantic problems. His friend obviously had no problem getting dates, but perhaps keeping a woman close to him was another issue. She said farewell to Mac and tried not to think too much about his strange behavior around his friend – or about the ring still locked safely away in her apartment upstairs.

Brenda still had a lot to do and was busy for the rest of the day with her guests. By early evening, all the guests had checked into the inn, and everyone had gathered in the sitting room for some coffee before dinner. The group was comprised of people of various ages and occupations and they were engaged in lively conversations. Brenda tapped a teaspoon against her coffee cup to get their attention.

"Good evening, everyone. Thank you for coming to the Sheffield Bed and Breakfast, we are all so pleased to have you here as our guests for the Sweetfern Harbor sailboat races. Just to let you know, there are two options for dinner tonight. You may choose to have dinner in the dining room here, or we can provide you with a complimentary ticket to the annual seafood dinner hosted by Morning Sun Coffee taking place tonight downtown. It is a fun night and almost like a street festival, so if you like a crowd or a party, it's definitely for you."

Allie added that Molly Lindsey, the housekeeper's daughter and owner of the coffee shop, had hired an Irish band to perform as entertainment. A traditional New England seafood buffet would be spread across a long table at the end of the shop with tables set up on the sidewalk and the street outside, which was cordoned off specially for the event. Brenda knew how delicious the seafood in Sweetfern Harbor was. She had never eaten fish as fresh as every bit she had enjoyed in this town.

"I understand the band will play fiddles," said Brenda. "There will also be a well-respected singer with the group." She turned to Phyllis. "Perhaps you can tell us more about your daughter's plans for the dinner event?"

Phyllis beamed as the gathered guests listened to her, rapt. "Molly expects the three captains to be there. You must meet them. The man who built their boats will be there, too. Wally Doyle's expertise in boat building is world renowned and he lives right here in Sweetfern Harbor."

The enthusiasm of the employees swept through the guests. The young couple stated they wanted to go but may not stay into the night, since they had the baby along. Allie pulled them aside when the group dispersed and told them she would be glad to watch the baby if they wanted to stay longer. It was agreed they would decide once the night moved along.

As it turned out, all the guests opted for the celebration at Morning Sun Coffee. They were in high spirits when they left the bed and breakfast to walk down to Main Street. Even from Sheffield House up the hill, the Irish music could be heard floating over the rooftops. Revelers were dancing in the street and bistro tables and chairs lined the sidewalk against the other shops. Brenda felt excited, too, as she would be free to attend the event now that her guests had all departed. Mac drove up to join her and escort her down to the seafood dinner, the merry sounds echoing through the little town announcing that the night was just beginning.

"How in the world does Molly manage to serve so many people from her shop?" Brenda asked as they walked.

"She enlists the help of every business owner in town. They all spare one or more of their employees to help her. Jenny told me she will switch off throughout the evening with one of her helpers in the flower shop. Molly clears everything in her kitchen to make room for extra food. The local appliance store lends extra refrigerators and a freezer for the event."

"Every space in her kitchen must be used in that case," Brenda marveled, shaking her head in amazement at Molly's ingenuity. Mac agreed. "Speaking of the flower shop...I haven't seen your daughter recently. How is she? I hope we run into her at some point."

"She's been very busy in the flower shop. Jenny's Blossoms has really taken off since William Pendleton started getting more events going. He knows how to draw crowds in. It's hard to believe how much this town has thrived since he took this upon himself. He sure blossomed after his wife died."

Brenda's thoughts switched to her housekeeper, whose romance with William had thrived once he had become a widower. Phyllis and William were a well-known item around town and she hoped they would tie the knot soon. Now that Phyllis had shared the news of Molly's engagement, maybe there would be a double wedding with mother and daughter sharing their special days.

"You're off in a cloud," said Mac. His teasing eyes brought Brenda back to the revelry around them. "We'd better hurry or every table will be filled."

"If the dinner is as delicious as I've heard I won't mind if I have to stand up and eat."

They waved back to old friends who greeted them as they passed and stood at the end of the line that wound a half block from the coffee shop door. Brenda spied Allie's mother, Hope Williams, going through the alley into the coffee shop. She carried a large box that Brenda knew contained either dessert pastries or some other delectable morsels from her bakery, Sweet Treats.

"After we finish with our dinner, I promised Molly I would help with some of the clean-up in her kitchen," Brenda said. "I have a feeling she'll be there late into the night getting things back in order."

"I'll go along with you and help as much as I can. There are more cops on duty tonight, but it won't surprise me if I get called for something."

"Do you have to worry about a lot of crime during the celebrations?"

"So far we've just had minor incidents. Usually it has something to do with too much drinking."

Finally, the line moved and they made it inside. The three captains' voices could be heard in the crowd. Wally was with them and they were in high spirits, bantering back and forth with one another. With large plates of food in hand, Brenda and Mac searched for a place to sit down, and found none available.

"Come on out here with us," said Captain Scully, spotting their looks of dismay. "We have dibs on a large table at the end of the block."

They followed him gratefully the short distance and Brenda saw the Reserved sign on the table that had kept the other guests at bay.

"Come on over here, young man," said Scully. "There's room for one more here."

Brenda turned quickly when she recognized Bryce's voice behind her.

"I have to be the luckiest guy in the world," he said with a smile as he walked up with his plate full. "I see that empty chair waiting just for me and it's next to a beautiful lady."

Several comments were made by Scully and Pratt that Bryce was indeed lucky. Brenda smiled back at him but moved her plate closer to Mac and shifted to make room for Bryce. Brenda couldn't help but wonder if some of the earlier tension would show itself between Mac and his old friend.

As she looked around, she realized why the captains chose this spot. They were near the little park where a large wooden dance floor had been set up. The band was tuning up and soon the music began. Crowds drew closer, some balanced their plates while they ate and others chose their dance partners. The captains' large table soon filled with hungry friends all chatting and watching the dancers. Brenda stated she had never eaten such delicious seafood. Everyone agreed. Bryce pushed his plate back when Brenda took her last bite.

"While Mac is finishing up, how about you and I get out there on that dance floor?" said Bryce.

Brenda looked at Mac and back at Bryce.

"I'm finished," said Mac simply, putting his fork down. "The first dance is mine." He looked at Bryce like a dare.

"Since I asked her first, I'm sure she will give me the honor," Bryce replied with a flashing look in his eyes.

Brenda sensed the tension was growing. "Both of you stop acting like schoolboys. I'll dance first with you, Bryce, since you asked first. It's only polite." She smiled at Mac. "You and I will be next out there and we'll show them how it's really done."

Dancing was something Brenda had enjoyed her entire life. Her father was quite the dancer and her mother had not been far behind him. They often danced at home when she was growing up, and as she listened to the lively Irish music, she could feel her feet itching to jump in.

"Well, Bryce, I hope you can keep up," she said with a grin as they joined the dancing crowds.

Once or twice she caught Mac's eye as they twirled around to the music. His face was impassive but his eyes were clouded with something she decided was jealousy. When Bryce pulled her closer than she wanted, she deftly stepped back from him while keeping time to the music. She smiled to herself when he missed a few steps.

The next piece was not as lively. Brenda was glad she saved that dance for Mac. He strode onto the dance floor and took her in his arms and she did not even see Bryce leave. She and Mac made perfect dancing partners. The crowd parted before them as if in admiration for the way they fit together.

"Aren't you happy I saved the slow dance for you?" She smiled up at him, hoping the cloud of jealousy would pass.

"I can't deny that."

"Tell me how you learned to dance like this," said Brenda, "I'm impressed, Mac Rivers."

That got him. He smiled a little as if proud to show off for her. "I didn't grow up knowing how to dance. But I soon learned in college that if I wanted to impress a girl at a party I'd better learn how. Once I took lessons I discovered I really liked it." He laughed. "Kept those lessons a secret. I took them in private and not even my roommates knew I was doing that."

"I don't care how you learned. I'm just glad you're good at it." As they swayed and turned to the slow song, she leaned her head onto his shoulder for a moment and felt so happy she could almost forget about the ring that wasn't on her finger at that moment.

They were both disappointed when the music ended. When they got back to their table, everyone congratulated them on their skills on the dance floor. Bryce was the only one who didn't hand out any compliments. Brenda started gathering up the paper plates, and Wally, Mac and Bryce stood to help her. They carried the plates to one of the large trash bins and dumped them in.

"We'd better get back to Molly's and help out as promised," said Brenda as they returned to the table.

Mac turned to the captains and bid them goodnight. "We'll see you in the morning around nine if that works for you. We're looking forward to touring your boats."

Bryce started to follow them to Molly's. But Mac's look convinced him to back off and he sat back down. There were few empty tables in town, a testament to the seafood dinner's success, and a mountain of pots and pans were waiting for them in the Morning Sun Coffee kitchen when they got there. By the time they finished washing up it was almost midnight. The evening had been a huge success and Molly and the rest of the workers received so many compliments that despite their tiredness, Brenda could see them glowing with contentment as Molly finally locked up the shop. The rest of the night would be enjoyed with dancing and impromptu parades in the streets, no matter how tired they were, because such a tremendous success deserved a tremendous celebration indeed.

chapter three

Brenda loved walking with Mac, especially in the nighttime. The smell of the ocean soothed her as they walked arm-in-arm down Main Street.

"This night always reminds me of Mardi Gras in New Orleans," said Mac. In the distance, they could still hear the music playing for a few last, diehard dancers. "I went down there one year and it was an experience of a lifetime for me. I never wanted to go back for it, but it sure was a fun time."

"I've never been down south at all. Maybe someday I will go down to the Florida beaches." She looked at Mac. "I'm bushed and ready to turn in for the night. How about you?"

"I agree. I'll walk you home. Be ready for me in the morning to pick you up for our boat tours. Does eight-thirty sound good?"

They agreed on the time and the closer they got to the bed and breakfast, the fainter the celebration sounds became. Mac stood inside the foyer with Brenda and took her into his arms for a farewell kiss before they parted. He held his lips on hers long enough to send shivers through her entire body and he still didn't let go of her. She finally pulled from him a few inches.

"As much as I hate to send you on your way, I really must. We have a full day tomorrow," she said reluctantly.

"I know. I know," he said. "It's just hard to let you go so easily." He told her goodnight and reached for the doorknob. Then he turned back impulsively and kissed her once more. After he left, Brenda felt his touch long into the night.

The next morning, Brenda told her chef Morgan to extend breakfast an extra half hour. "I'm sure everyone came in late last night and may sleep in a little longer this morning."

Morgan readily agreed. Phyllis took a bite of buttered toast. "It was a wonderful night. I'm so proud of William. He knows how to draw a crowd to our little village."

"I agree, he's done a lot for Sweetfern Harbor."

Phyllis left the table a few minutes later and stated she would start cleaning the sitting room first. "I doubt any of the rooms will be ready for cleaning until around noon or early afternoon."

Brenda agreed with her as she finished her coffee. But she hurried to her apartment when she realized Mac would be there to pick her up in fifteen minutes. No one on the second floor stirred as she quickly walked back to her apartment door and went in to reapply her make-up. Just as she was finishing up, she heard soft voices in the foyer. She recognized his voice and she couldn't help but feel that special feeling inside – but she had to force herself not to glance longingly at the drawer where the ring lay hidden in its box. Mac Rivers stood waiting for her.

Phyllis told Brenda she would watch the front desk since Allie had babysat late the night before and would be in at ten. Brenda thanked her for pitching in to help and then she and Mac left.

"I can't wait to tour a racing boat," said Brenda with excitement.

Mac opened his car door for her and they headed for the docks. As he drove down Main Street, they noticed two of the captains entering the coffee shop and he slowed the car down. "We'd better stop and let them know we're on our way now. I wonder if they expected to be there when we look at the boats."

He parked and they walked across the street to the shop. Scully and Pratt were chatting with David Williams, the boat race official. David said hello to Brenda and Mac, as did the captains.

"We're on our way to tour your boats. Do you prefer we wait for you to go with us?" Brenda asked.

"The boats are unlocked. We don't mind if you take a self-tour. Let the man at the harbor know it's all right with us." Captain Pratt then mentioned that Captain Eddy was probably down there. "Tell him hello for me. It will probably be hard for him to lose but that's the way it goes." He laughed as if he had told the joke of a lifetime.

Mac took Brenda's arm and told everyone they would see them at the race. When they got to the harbor, they were astounded at the sight of the three boats a few yards from one another.

"Once again Wally has outdone himself," said Mac, taking in the sight of the trim sailboats shining in the sun and bobbing gently on the water. They were elegant crafts that looked as if they were racing even when they were at anchor, with deeply polished sides and decks, shiny brass fittings, and crisp sails and ropes stretching up to their tall masts. "I heard it took him two years to build these three new boats. From the outside, it doesn't look as if he shortchanged the captains on anything."

"You are so right. They are spectacular." Brenda shielded her eyes with her right hand and scanned the harbor. She stopped at the Eddy. "I guess Captain Eddy is in his boat."

"He may be, or he could be enjoying the town and his fans

here to watch him win. I know the competitors always like to mingle with the crowds around Sweetfern Harbor before the race starts." He took her hand. "Let's start with the Eddy. We might get a personal tour from Captain Eddy if he's here."

They walked the short pier to the docked Eddy. At close range, it was even more dazzling than it was from a distance. They knocked on the door of the cabin. Brenda waited with excitement and looked around the harbor again. But then, strangely, they realized no one was answering their knock. When Mac knocked harder the second time, the door pushed open under his hand. He looked at Brenda and then called out to Captain Eddy. There was no response. They looked at each other questioningly.

"I suppose we can go on in. He did tell us last night to take a look at his boat, too," Brenda said. "It's like you said. He's probably mingling with the tourists in town."

They entered and the richly detailed mahogany interior impressed Brenda. "This wood is beautiful." They looked around at the neat cabinetry and upholstered seats with nautical motifs embroidered along the edges. "Do you think there's a sleeping cabin on board?" She looked around, curious about everything she saw.

"Oh yes, definitely. I think these captains often take long voyages together. They will be on the water for days or weeks at a time."

"Do they go in one boat together?"

"As I understand it, they each run their own boat but follow the same route. I've often wondered how they know how to navigate like that together."

Mac led the way and they found the cabin where the captain slept. Brenda excitedly peered around from behind the detective, eager to see the cozy sleeping cabin. But she saw two feet at the end of the bed and she stepped back, embarrassed.

"Let's not wake him. We can go to the other two boats and come back when he wakes up."

But Mac didn't budge. Captain Eddy's clothing appeared wet from the waist up. One of his hands laid over the other one, unnaturally still. Too still to be sleeping. Mac walked closer and Brenda followed him. He felt the captain's pulse and then turned to Brenda and shook his head.

"I'll call for an ambulance," Mac said, "but I don't think he will need CPR."

Shock waves shot through Brenda. She stared at the still form on the bed. His physique looked massive compared to her observations of him in the coffee shop, but in death, he was utterly motionless. She stepped away and waited numbly for Mac to make his call. After that was done, they walked up onto the deck. Both knew to observe, not touch. Brenda pointed to a large open-topped barrel filled with water. There were faint red streaks on the side of the wooden vessel.

"Could that be blood?" said Brenda. "Do you think this was foul play?"

"I have my suspicions. It looked like he had been positioned and his upper clothing was damp. The rest of him was dry."

Brenda formed her next words carefully.

"I think he must have been killed right here on the deck," Brenda said. "The blood is probably the result of scraping his hands to fight off whoever was dunking his head in this water." She bent down and examined the red marks closely and saw what might be scratches incised into the wet wood. She felt certain the marks were streaks of blood.

"Your premise is believable, especially knowing his clothing is wet only on the top half. If he had drowned in the harbor, or somewhere else of natural causes, he would be wet head to toe. I think whoever killed him dragged him up to his bed."

They stepped back when they heard the sirens. Two officers appeared on the deck behind two EMTs who were quickly directed to the bed in the cabin. Mac immediately went into professional mode and ordered the cops to start taping off the boat and then begin taking samples from what he determined was the initial scene of the act. He made a grim phone call to the county offices and soon the coroner arrived and he quickly pronounced Captain Eddy deceased.

"It looks like a drowning," the coroner said as he filled out his paperwork, "but it's curious that only his upper clothing is wet. That obviously means he didn't fall overboard."

Brenda watched as the coroner consulted with Mac and the police officers began to comb over the crime scene meticulously. Her mind flooded with possibilities of who could have done such a thing. Mac seemed to read her thoughts as he paused and came to her side.

"It's a mystery as to who could have done this...and what was the motive? He seemed like a likeable guy and compared to the other two, he didn't even speak up much." He shook his head.

Brenda had no answer and she continued to observe the surroundings, trying to keep out of the way. She knew Mac needed her to make a witness statement, but she nervously glanced at her watch. The races were scheduled to begin at noon, which meant in a short time, the crowds would be in place to watch an event that probably wouldn't happen. It would be a madhouse. She felt a sinking feeling in the pit of her stomach as she realized her beloved town of Sweetfern Harbor had been touched again by a deadly crime.

"Maybe we should contact Captains Scully and Pratt," she said.

"I think we'll wait for a few more minutes. I don't want them to burst in here until we finish preliminary work. Once Captain Eddy's body is off the boat, I'll do that personally. Do you want to go along with me?"

"Yes, I do. They will be very upset. They were like brothers from what everyone has said." She recalled how much they enjoyed bantering with one another last night. A huge hole would be left between them when they heard the news.

Sometime later, it was finally determined the body could be removed, and the coroner and his technicians slowly wheeled the body to their van, wrapped carefully in a white sheet. As usual, word had already spread through Sweetfern Harbor about the death of Captain Eddy. Just as the coroner's gurney reached the van parked at the docks, the two captains rushed to the harbor and Mac and Brenda had to intercept them before they reached the boat of their fallen brother. Pratt and Scully stood stock-still in shock at the news, as the body was wheeled past them. Pratt spoke first.

"I can't believe Eddy is dead. Our brother, our fellow captain. What happened?"

"Everything is preliminary at this point," Mac said. "As soon as we know anything we'll put out the word. I'm very sorry for your loss. I know how much he meant to both of you."

The captains thanked him for his kind words, their eyes distant. Then Captain Scully seemed to rouse himself and said something surprising to both Brenda and the detective.

"David Williams says the race will proceed," he said. "There's a visiting detective – a friend of yours, apparently? – who says he knows how to race a sailboat. He grew up around here, and he says he will take Eddy's place in the race."

Mac stared at Captain Scully in disbelief. "This is a crime scene. No one is racing this boat any time soon. They will have to at least delay the race until later this afternoon. We need time to go over this boat and can't risk losing fingerprints and other evidence that is here. During a race, a lot of the forensic evidence will be contaminated or lost completely."

"Detective Bryce Jones assures us forensics can finish in a short time frame," said a voice behind them. Mac and Brenda turned to see David Williams approaching them from the parking lot at the docks. He had a grim but determined look on his face. "The race must go on. The town can't afford to lose money on this. If the top seeded competitors – that's the Eddy, the Scully, and the Pratt – if they don't race, the town is liable for refunds for everyone who purchased a ticket. I'm sorry. This is a true tragedy but we can't make it worse by plunging the town into bankruptcy. We'd never be able to afford to continue the race in the future. As sad as it is, today the race must go on." David Williams stood behind the two captains and clapped their shoulders briefly as if in solidarity. Brenda was taken aback and she scrutinized the two captains' faces, curious to see their reaction. But both men must've still been in shock. They betrayed no signs of grief. Only the blank looks of men staring out at the coroner's van as it drove away.

Mac clamped his lips tight and then said "David, I understand what you're saying, but you have to understand that Detective Jones does not have any jurisdiction in this investigation. He has no idea how long we'll need and he has no right giving you a timeline. This is a crime scene and can't be rushed through. I'm prepared to go before a judge if you want to take issue with the police department's authority on this matter, but for now, I am in charge and you will have to delay things until we are finished."

David's eyes held onto Mac's. Brenda noticed the race official was first to look away. "Fine, I'll go get a judge. Perhaps you don't understand how important this race is. Bryce Jones is a fine detective and perhaps you should learn a thing or two about crime scene processing from someone like him," David finished, letting his insult land with devastating force. Mac's stare penetrated the man in front of him. David pressed on. "If Jones knows how to race then he will be the one racing this boat." He turned on his heel and left.

Mac didn't say anything. Brenda felt his anger seething through his skin. She found it hard to believe the audacity of Detective Bryce Jones. He should know his place in this serious situation. She wondered just how good a detective he was in Brooklyn if he came back to Sweetfern Harbor, his own hometown, just to get involved in a mess like this.

"What can I do to speed things along in case they recklessly go ahead with this race?" Brenda asked Mac.

"I wish I could say that no judge will allow this. I wish I knew which one David will go to. He has an edge with the court system. Some in there go way back with him." Mac led the way back to the sailboat as he told her several things that must be done first. She worked alongside the cops who specialized in forensics as they worked on the most urgent tasks. Frustratingly, no fingerprints had showed up in their initial sweep of the crime scene. There were more advanced techniques they could try, but that would take time. Meanwhile, Mac went to speak to the two captains who now stood behind the yellow tape at the entrance to the boat.

"This race must go forward, Detective," said Scully. "Eddy wouldn't want it any other way."

"We have a crime scene here. He did not die a natural death. At best, the race will be delayed. I'm not even promising we'll be finished by noon." Mac found it hard to believe the two were focused more on the race than on the death of their friend and competitor, but before he could pose a question to them about their attitude, another pair of police cars pulled up nearby. He left the captains for the moment and went around to one side of the car to instruct the new arrivals as to where they were needed.

"David is going on TV just now," said one of the younger cops who just arrived. "He's asking for anyone who knows how to race a boat like this to step forward. That's in case someone is better than Bryce Jones. But I think we all know Jones was good at it when he lived here a while back. He knows what he's doing out on the water." Just as he said this, Mac stepped around the boat to where they were chatting.

Mac glared at the man, who looked away and shuffled his feet. Mac gave him orders to get busy on forensics in the cargo hold with one of the older cops. Brenda was sure the young cop was directed to someone more experienced and mature. At any rate, she knew his words didn't set well with the detective.

chapter four

M ac quietly fumed as he returned to the sailboat to continue with the investigation that was now under the pressure of a ludicrous deadline. He knew Bryce was an expert, but he had no right to step in like this – and he certainly wasn't acting like much of a friend. The young detective was brash and assuming, something that did not tone down Detective Mac Rivers' mood.

Mac and his crew continued to gather forensic evidence on Captain Eddy's boat. Even in a trying situation, the detective was proud of his team of officers because they took their jobs seriously, and several were experts in forensics. However, it was a race against time. If they just had more time, he could get a more detailed fingerprint scan completed.

"We'll stay here until we're forced off by a higher authority," said Mac when several officers asked him about the timeline. His words were barely spoken when Detective Bryce Jones appeared at the cabin door. He started to lift the tape. "Stop right there, Bryce. This is not your jurisdiction and you have not been invited to help with the investigation."

Bryce's face held a calm smile that disturbed Brenda. He waved a paper in Mac's view. "I'm not here about the investigation. It seems the judge agreed with David Williams that the race should go forward. I'm here to look over the controls of this magnificent boat. Would you ever have thought in our youth that I'd one day get to man such a vessel? And to think I'll be racing it in one of the most prestigious races of all." It appeared Bryce was focused on one issue only.

Mac snatched the paper from his hand and flipped it open. He stuffed it in his shirt pocket without a word. "We'll be off the boat in time for the race to go as planned. You can learn the boat's controls when we're finished moving the equipment."

Bryce grinned and winked at Brenda before he left.

"I can't believe a judge would allow this before the crime scene is done," said Brenda. "No court of law will accept any evidence we collect after the race because the crime scene will be contaminated." And privately, she thought, no decent person should be so excited about racing another when it came at the cost of another man's death. Was Bryce being naïve, or was there something more going on here?

"I agree with you," Mac was saying as he began packing up, "but it's out of my hands now. I just hope we will be able to solve this crime based on the evidence we've already gathered." Mac ordered the officers to gather what they had and make sure it was all labeled correctly. Then he told the man with the camera to get photos of every nook and cranny. "That includes the deck especially and the cabin where the body was found. According to the judge's order, we have to be off the boat shortly."

Brenda recalled how fit Captain Eddy had been. If one person carried him, that person was also fit, and strong. "It's hard to imagine someone carrying a body like Captain Eddy without dragging it along the deck. He was strong and fit. I don't recall seeing any drag marks, so maybe it was two people."

She tried not to imagine Captains Scully and Pratt doing anything like this to the man they seemed to love. Both were strong enough, but her stomach churned to think of the captains hiding such a deadly secret beneath their long history of friendship. Surely it had to have been someone just as strong as they were, though.

"I just don't know at this point," Mac said. "I have to agree with your conclusions. I'm told there are no signs of someone being dragged to the cabin. Maybe we'll find something in the little time we have left. We have to get as much done as possible before we have to leave this boat." He walked off with his brow furrowed, inspecting the corners the crime scene photographer had captured.

They did the best they could, but it wasn't long before the race officials appeared with another copy of the judge's order and ushered the entire police crew off. As they unloaded bags of evidence and their equipment, Bryce pushed past them like a kid in a candy shop. He didn't meet either Mac's or Brenda's eyes. Instead, he hurried to the front of the boat where he started inspecting the sails and then sat down and began examining the controls at the helm. Mac shook his head in disgust. Brenda was appalled that his friend was acting so callously in this situation and wondered if his behavior made Mac as suspicious as she was starting to become of his motives.

"You find a place to watch the races," Mac said to Brenda as he loaded everything into the trunk of a police car. "Try to get a seat where you can observe as many people as possible. I'm going to mingle through the crowds and will stick close to the finish line to be there when the race ends."

Brenda found a strategic spot that gave her the opportunity to observe most of the crowd below her. She barely had time to process what had happened that morning. It seemed half the crowd was gossiping about the death, and half the crowd was blithely celebrating as if nothing had happened at all. Everyone cheered and clapped when the three boats lined up alongside a few amateur sailboats that would also take part, even though they knew they had no hope of competing with the three headliners. The captains waved to the crowds on shore and Brenda could see Bryce beaming as bright as the sun that overlooked the stunning boats and the sparkling ocean as the crowd cheered wildly.

Still, the events of the morning seemed to lodge in her gut like a seasickness. Something was not right, and the uneasy feeling Brenda felt caused her stomach to lurch. Her eyes went to David Williams as he stood on the race officials' platform and held the starting gun in the air. The captains were in position, hands poised on the ropes of their sails, and David fired the gun. Brenda's eyes were glued to the sailboats, whose sails suddenly unfurled as they leapt into motion. Sun glistened on the waters and the superb boats were so beautiful and fast she caught her breath. The painting she had seen did not do justice to the real spectacle in front of her.

Brenda found herself caught up in the race as the crowds thrilled. There were a lot of cheers when Bryce sped ahead of the two seasoned captains for the first half of the race. The buoys that marked the race were bright orange and looped far out into the harbor bay, and as the sailboats sped along their course, some spectators pulled out binoculars to continue watching the farthest part of the race until the boats turned to come back to the harbor for the finish line. Momentarily she wished for a pair of binoculars of her own, forgetting Mac's instructions to her. She remembered with a start, and scanned the people near her who were all shouting encouragement to their favorites. A voice behind her talked loudly to his friend to be heard over the roar of the spectators.

"I wonder what happened to Captain Eddy," the man said. "I thought he always raced his own boat."

The man with him answered just as loudly. "I hope he isn't sick or something. I had all my bets on Eddy. No idea who this new guy is or if they'll honor a bet on the sailboat if it's got a new captain."

Brenda adjusted her sunglasses and saw the boats had now turned on their course back towards the harbor where they were easier to see. The crowd swelled with agonized cheers as the Eddy was slowly but steadily beginning to lose its lead. Then Bryce tacked around one buoy too widely, and there was a great shout from the crowd as the Scully and then the Pratt overtook him, their sails straining to catch the fierce winds out on the bay. The Scully and the Pratt were now neck-and-neck for the lead! The Sweetfern Harbor throng loudly encouraged the new captain of the Eddy to catch up, happy to be rooting for the underdog.

"What's wrong with him?" yelled a woman in front of Brenda.

Others chimed in until a man shouted. "Something's wrong with that boat!" He was staring intently into his binoculars. "Oh my gosh...he's taking on water. I'm sure it's sinking. Look at the way it's slowly going down." The woman next to him didn't believe him. He handed her the binoculars. "Look for yourself." More and more people were turning away from watching the Scully and the Pratt racing toward the finish line to watch as Bryce frantically waved his arms for help, holding the radio in one hand.

Brenda's gut lurched again. Something was definitely wrong with the Eddy. It now sat perilously low in the water. For a few moments, the crowd was tense with silence, waiting for someone to step in. Brenda immediately looked over to the officials' platform where she saw David Williams tweaking his earphones off his head as panic swept across his face. Brenda decided to carefully make her way close enough to the officials' platform to hear more of what was going on. A second later, she saw David speak to his co-officials and hurry from his vantage point on the platform. Most people still watched the activities out on the water, while others focused on David Williams. When he rushed past Brenda, she heard him speak into his headset.

"Bryce is calling for help. His boat is sinking. Get someone out there immediately."

Brenda left her position and raced to keep up with David. "What's going on?"

David shook his head. "I don't know. Bryce signaled an S.O.S. and said the boat is sinking fast. I have no idea what happened."

In the meantime, Mac had realized right away something was wrong out on the water. He raced to the rescue crew waiting near the finish line and boarded the speedboat with the medics and rescue team that sped to the scene. Brenda stood helplessly on the sand and noticed Captain Scully had unexpectedly pulled his sails sharply to the side and was turning his boat around. Both captains must have heard Bryce's call for help on their radios. Scully reached Bryce on the Eddy seconds before the rescue boat arrived.

Behind Brenda, the crowd stepped out of the stands and moved closer to the edge of the ocean.

"Look at Pratt," said a man. "He's still heading to the finish line." There were hushed sounds of disbelief from the crowd.

Brenda stared in horror as Captain Pratt ignored the disaster behind him and crossed the finish line at full speed. He dropped his sails and slowed down and coasted smoothly in to the docks by the racing officials' stand. But only some in the crowd remained cheering for his empty triumph, and the celebratory mood of the spectators seemed to be muted.

While the onlookers' attention was divided between the finish line and the rescue activities, David Williams had returned to his post and pronounced Captain Pratt the winner, his voice echoing over the harbor on the loudspeakers. Captain Pratt lifted the silver cup high in the air for the press photographers and signed some autographs. From a distance, his face was unreadable to Brenda.

Brenda turned to look as Captain Scully's boat glided back into harbor, followed by the rescue boat zooming back to shore. Bryce stepped onto the docks looking shaken but safe, wrapped in a blanket from the medics. Mac conferred with the rescue personnel briefly and then radioed all officers in the area to come to a designated location for further orders. Brenda hurried to join them.

Mac walked toward her and pointed to the waters. "There goes the entire crime scene."

"It's unbelievable. There's just no way it was a coincidence, Mac."

"Whatever happened to sink that boat must relate to the murder of Captain Eddy," said Mac. "Someone wants to make sure it will be impossible to solve this case."

They both watched the crowds gather around Bryce and Captain Scully as they reached the docks and stood for photographs. Reporters peppered them all with questions and seemed to have as many for the winner, Captain Pratt, as they did for the rescuer Captain Scully and the newly minted Captain Bryce Jones with his tragically sunk boat. Brenda shook her head. Everything proceeded as if the earlier events of the day had never happened.

"It's no use talking to Scully and Jones now," said Mac. "As soon as the crowds let them go, I'm bringing both of them in for statements. I have to get to the bottom of all of this. In the meantime, I have officers interviewing everyone they see. If anyone appears to know anything in the least, they are to be brought in for further questioning."

Brenda touched his arm, sensing the tension that was

gathering in him as this difficult case became more complex by the minute. "Let me know if you need me later today." She told him of the conversations overheard behind her. "Not everyone knows that Captain Eddy was murdered." Mac took this in and grasped her hand with his. "I have to head back to the bed and breakfast now. Practically the whole town will be there soon for the celebratory lunch, as is tradition. Phyllis is mostly in charge but I still have a lot of details to oversee. When you get the photos from the crime scene I would appreciate a call from you. Do you mind?"

For the first time in several hours, Mac smiled at her. "I don't mind at all. I value your input. You know you're my secret weapon." He squeezed her hand again briefly and then turned to address his team of officers who had gathered in the parking lot. She turned to walk back to the Sheffield House as quickly as she could, knowing she still had a busy day ahead of her.

By the time she returned, all the guests had arrived at the bed and breakfast after the race, and almost all of the luncheon guests were lined up on the lawn at the long tables or grouped around the gardens chatting and eating. Brenda's staff were overwhelmed and she pitched in immediately, becoming so busy that she barely had time to think. Chef Morgan had prepared the lunch just as she did every year after the annual boat race. Tickets were snapped up in advance since everyone knew they were guaranteed a gourmet spread of hot and cold barbecue sandwiches, numerous salads, tasty desserts, and her famous lemonade and home brewed iced tea. Over the years it had grown to be such a big event that everyone at the Sheffield pitched in, including the owner. Brenda was refilling the lemonade dispenser when she fumbled for her cell phone as it rang.

"I've asked Molly to help at the bed and breakfast," said Mac. "I know you are busier than ever today. She'll be right there and she's bringing Jenny, too."

"Thank you, Mac. This is bigger than I expected and we need all the help we can get. Have you had a chance to talk with Bryce and Scully?"

"They're on their way now, I'll fill you in after."

Brenda focused on the influx of people in her bed and breakfast. All thoughts of helping Mac at this point proved impossible. The lunch guests buzzed about the events as she moved about the lawn helping her staff. A few comments were overheard that voiced opinions as to whether Pratt should have kept going.

"I don't think it was a fair win," said a woman. She looked to be in her early thirties and Brenda wondered if she knew Bryce Jones. The man next to her seemed to agree. "I mean," she continued, "he should have gone back to help like Scully did. It's just good sportsmanship. What fun is it to win a race against no other competitors?"

Others were less interested in the strange finish than they were in its unusual start. When someone mentioned the death of Captain Eddy, all attention became riveted on the speaker. Brenda didn't bother trying to calm the rumors. Nothing she could do would change the way any of them thought about the entire affair. She busied herself in the hope that no one would ask her opinion about the death of someone they admired, and tried to shake from her mind that image of Captain Eddy dead in his cabin berth. Brenda went into the kitchen to check with Chef Morgan. Things were proceeding in an orderly fashion and Brenda breathed thanks for her good employees.

As the afternoon wore on, the diners moved to the gardens and the staff cleared the long tables. There was no formal end time to the luncheon and the guests were free to mingle on the grounds. Some drifted into the sitting room while others sat at the long dining room table to continue their conversations. As they finished eating and talking, the guests trickled back toward the downtown area until the Sheffield Bed and Breakfast began to feel normal again.

"I can't tell you how much the two of you are appreciated," Brenda said. She smiled at Jenny and Molly.

"We all have to work together in Sweetfern Harbor," said Jenny as she carried one last tub of dishes to the kitchen. "It's been quite a weekend. My dad has a lot of work ahead of him. I don't expect to see him around home much for the next week or so."

"He'll get to the bottom of things," said Molly. "Are you going to help out with this strange case, Brenda?"

"I have told him if he needs me to do anything on it, I'll be available. I was there with him on the boat this morning, as he probably told you, Jenny. But he probably won't need me until tomorrow. I'm pretty worn out after today."

"The two of you make a good team," said Jenny with a grin. She liked the pretty owner of the bed and breakfast and was pleased that her widower father had found love later in life with Brenda. "Is there anything else we can do here?"

"I think that's it. I'll check in the kitchen to see how it's going in there. Thank you again."

As Brenda stretched across her bed hours later, fully clothed, her cell rang.

"We have the pictures printed and blown up," said Mac, sounding just as tired as she felt. "The Chief and I are putting them in order. It's going to be a long night and I know you've had quite a day. We should have things ready in the morning if you want to come down and take a look. We need your input since you were right there at the scene."

"I'll be there. I still can't believe the judge ruled so quickly to let the race go forward. But I guess there's nothing to be done about that now."

Mac mumbled something under his breath and ended the call. Brenda got his message loud and clear. Mac Rivers was not a fan of this judge, whoever he or she was.

. . .

The next morning, Brenda awoke to find the summer sun shining in her curtains, but she found herself wishing for another few hours of rest. Instead of the murder and the sunken sailboat, she found herself thinking back to Mac's proposal to her, and his strange reluctance to announce it afterward. It seemed like an event now buried under the pressing call of solving the murder of Captain Eddy. She resolved that if she could not fully understand Mac's heart, at least she could help him with his investigation.

Brenda gave careful instructions to her staff and left for the police station. Anxious to see the photos, she almost ran the one light between Sheffield Bed and Breakfast and the police station in town. She slammed on the brakes and gasped, but luckily no one was around. The town was relatively quiet the morning after the race. When she got to the station, by contrast, it was very busy. Several officers came and went through the front door. When she walked up the steps, one stood back and held it open for her, then hurried out to his patrol car with a folder in his hand. She supposed they were chasing down all available leads right now.

She found Mac and Chief Bob Ingram in his office. Mac handed her a coffee and refilled his own. The Chief declined more coffee when asked, and wearily rubbed his eyes as if he had barely slept. In front of them on a table were spread the blown-up photographs of the crime scene and the body itself.

"Fill Brenda in on what you have so far," said Mac.

"There's no doubt in my mind," said the Chief, "that Captain Eddy's head was submerged under water, most likely the water in that wooden barrel we saw on the Eddy's deck. It wasn't a quick death, either." The Chief grimaced as he pulled one photo to the top of the stack. Brenda looked on, carefully controlling her expression. "He fought to stay alive. You can see it in the pictures, too, but the autopsy confirmed it after examination of his right hand. His fingernails were torn up and he has long scratch marks to the wrist." The Chief looked away then, and they were all quiet for a moment as the gravity of the crime hit them. "We have to catch the lowlife who did this to Captain Eddy," he finished, dropping the photo back on the pile as he sat back wearily in his chair.

chapter five

The photos in front of her mesmerized Brenda, as gory as they were. In blown-up form, she was able to look at the crime scene in a detached manner. It was easier than it had been when she was physically there. She barely heard Mac's voice. "Whoever did this carried his body to his cabin and positioned him on his bunk." Mac looked at Brenda, who remained transfixed on the photos. He explained that the police were working on a plan to try to raise the sailboat from the bottom of the harbor, but it would take some time, and there was no guarantee that it would yield any additional evidence anyway.

She finally looked up at the men. "With no fingerprints and a lost crime scene, we have only his body and these photos." She crossed her arms and leaned back against the desk behind her. "I still think it had to be two people. You said there were no drag marks along the floors. How could one person have carried his body to his cabin and placed him in the bed? Do we have any early leads on a suspect or suspects?" Both men shook their heads in the negative.

"I agree it either took one very hearty person, or two, to move the body that far from the deck." The Chief looked again at the photos. "But that gets us no closer to figuring out who it was. Do you see anything new this morning, Brenda?"

She leaned forward to shuffle through the enlarged photos and examine the details. "It all looks the same as we saw it when we discovered the body. There just wasn't anything left behind that was obvious. I think interviews will be the best way to crack this case. The throng of people who were here won't make it very easy." She leaned back and looked at Mac and the Chief. "I think it was someone right here in Sweetfern Harbor. Statistically, it's more likely to be someone who knew him well, right? He's lived here his whole life. The only thing that would change my mind is if someone from the outside held a grudge against Captain Eddy. If so, it would have been something very significant. Also, the dock where the racing boats were moored is practically in the center of town. There's not a lot of places to hide. So, whoever boarded Eddy's boat didn't cause any suspicion around the harbor." The Chief grimaced when she said this. They were all thinking the same thing – it seemed like all evidence was pointing towards the other captains.

Brenda pulled out her phone. She said the names out loud as she typed them in a short list. Captain Eddy's two competitors came first. Then she put in Bryce Jones' name and David Williams. She knew they had no evidence to pin the crime on any of them, but they were the closest ones associated with the boat race and the death. Then she put in Wally Doyle's name, remembering his friendly relationship with the captains at the seafood dinner in town a few nights before.

"There's a lot of work to do on this case," said Mac. "Scully and Pratt called the county coroner and said they want his body released so they can have him cremated and his ashes returned to the sea. That can't happen until we find his next of kin, who may have other ideas."

"Or until we find a will," Brenda pointed out. "It may tell

us who stood to inherit anything of value he may have owned...other than the sunken boat, of course."

"I have officers already out there questioning anyone they can find. We have to know if anyone saw something suspicious around the boats the night before or morning before the race." Mac slapped the new folder on his desk. "We'll get to the bottom of this no matter what. By tomorrow I want to start questioning everyone on that list." He looked at Brenda with a question in his eyes. She nodded yes and agreed she would help out.

"Good," said the Chief. "Tonight, as crazy as it seems, the closing firework display for the boat race will go on as planned. The spectators will be there in throngs. Keep your eyes and ears open. My men will be watching but we should keep our eyes and ears peeled."

Brenda left the police station turning this all over in her mind. She flashed back to prior investigations that she had helped Mac with, where the deceased person had many enemies, but this one just didn't seem to make sense. What enemies did a kindly, quiet old racing boat captain have? Just as she got to her car, she heard a familiar voice.

"How about going to the fireworks with me tonight, Brenda?" Bryce Jones leaned against his rental car with his legs crossed, waiting for her answer. "I'd love to be seen with Sweetfern Harbor's own attractive female sleuth on my arm." He gave her one of his trademark brilliant smiles and she struggled not to roll her eyes a little.

"I don't think so, Bryce. Mac and I will be going together, I'm sure. I know he plans to go and we do things together..."

Bryce's expression soured a little bit as he stood up straighter, his charming poise gone for the moment. "I'm sure you think you are the only one in Mac's eyes. As a matter of fact, he has dated many beautiful women. You aren't the first one since his wife's death ten years ago and I doubt you'll be the last." He gave her a half-smile as he watched her unlock her door. "Consider this a fair warning. He hops from girl to girl faster than the waves on the ocean in a storm."

"Thanks for the advice, but I know you are wrong in this case." She got into her car and drove off before he had time to answer. She willed her hands to stop shaking on the steering wheel. If only he wasn't staying in her bed and breakfast, this would be so much easier, Brenda thought.

Back at the bed and breakfast, Brenda walked in to hear guests and staff alike buzzing with excitement. Everyone was moving to the terrace where Chef Morgan had set out a light lunch for the guests. All talked of the upcoming fireworks finale to the unusual annual boat race later that night. A few minutes later, Bryce Jones came in. He smiled at Brenda as several guests crowded around him to talk about his ordeal on the water. She steeled herself not to react to his presence.

"It's a wonder you didn't go down with the boat," said one guest.

"I'm an expert swimmer," he said, "but I have to admit, it was a scary few minutes. A sinking boat can pull you down in its wake very easily. When I saw the rescue boat coming out and Captain Scully turn around, I knew I'd make it out alive. I didn't even know Pratt kept going until later. I don't hold that against the man. He knew I was in good hands with Scully and someone had to keep going to win it."

Brenda could not listen to another word and instead retreated to the kitchen to consult with her chef. She closed the kitchen door to the voices that relived the earlier events. She knew she would have to interrogate Bryce Jones one-on-one, and probably before the fireworks that night. Despite her promise to help Mac, she wondered if it was a good idea to be interrogating one of her own guests. Not to mention that she did not look forward to Mac and Bryce airing any more of their jealous disagreements.

Lunch finished and everyone moved inside to the sitting room for dessert. Brenda joined them again. She felt Bryce's eyes on her several times during dessert but chose to ignore him. Instead, she concentrated on the young couple seated to her right. The baby sat on her father's lap while he balanced a brownie in his other hand. Everyone voiced how good the child had been. She appeared happy all the time and provided added entertainment for guests. Talk of the fireworks display was the foremost topic of conversation. Bryce interjected some of the history of boat race events and Phyllis and a few other staff members chimed in.

Brenda realized that perhaps she could avoid Mac's uncomfortable interview session with Bryce at the police station if she simply sat down with him at the bed and breakfast. Brenda ran several questions through her mind that she intended to ask Bryce when he finished his last bite of chocolate cake.

He excused himself, along with several others, and Brenda followed him to the foyer. "I want to ask you about some details about the race yesterday." He seemed much more relaxed after chatting with the other guests and turned his charm on her full force. She smiled back a little bit, hoping they could forget about the earlier incident in the parking lot.

"Of course, Brenda. I wondered why you seemed so distracted over dessert. I'll be glad to be interrogated by one of the best. Shall we?"

They went into the small library down the hall and Brenda brought her phone out. She started with the first inquiry on her list.

"Where were you the morning of the race?"

Bryce grew serious. "I was at Morning Sun Coffee with the captains, I listened to Wally describe how he built the boats. I was fascinated. I just wanted to get a tour, but who knew I'd be the captain of one of those boats a few hours later."

"Did you hear anyone say anything that might make sense of the crime now?"

He shook his head. "I've gone over those very things in

my own mind. There was nothing out of the ordinary. The two captains jabbed at one another the way they had been doing every time they had an audience." His eyes grew fond as he recalled the moment, then he seemed distant. He sat up straighter and snapped his fingers. "Wait. Captain Pratt mentioned Eddy more than once. He kept wondering where Eddy was. Scully gave him a couple of icy stares, but I figured Pratt was getting on his nerves. Maybe Pratt was trying to build up an alibi, maybe not. Maybe Scully knew something, maybe not. But if it were my case, I'd definitely put that one in my file for future reference."

"We're all very glad you weren't hurt in the accident. Since the boat sank, there isn't much to go on except the photos and the autopsy report. We already checked the harbor and there were definitely no rocks near the race course. But did you hear any unusual sounds before the boat started taking on water?"

"Not really. The wind is pretty loud when you're racing out on the water, but I think I would have noticed if I'd hit something. I noticed a little water and at first didn't realize the boat was leaking. I thought maybe a wave had just come over the side. But then the water came in faster as if a hole widened. That's when I raced to the front to radio for help." Brenda thought she saw a fleeting fear cross his face. "If you want suspects, I'd look at Wally Doyle. The captains knew everything about sailing, but he knows everything about building boats."

"Mac and the Chief are pulling in everyone they feel has some input at the moment. I'm sure you'll be called back." For the first time, Brenda realized the handsome detective could be professional when called for.

"That's to be expected. I'm sticking around for a few extra days or as long as needed." Just as suddenly as the sober, professional detective had appeared, Bryce switched back to being a flirt. "Too bad you aren't going with me tonight. I could show you a good time in Sweetfern Harbor. I know every nook and cranny around here." He smiled as he tried to tempt her, and she couldn't help but smile back, even though she was a little exasperated by his relentless flirting. Brenda felt relief he didn't mention Mac's past girlfriends again. For the moment, all she knew was that Bryce Jones was someone she could easily dismiss. She thanked him for the interview and left to call Mac from the privacy of her apartment.

"Your voice is music to my ears and came at the right time. This case is frustrating," said Mac. He relayed that the officers who had fanned out all over town interviewing tourists had not turned up anything useful so far. Meanwhile, Eddy had no next of kin except some distant cousins who were willing to go along with Pratt and Scully's plans for the body, and no large assets had turned up in their searches. That eliminated one line of investigation: no one had killed him for his money. His boat had been his only real asset and the boat insurance policy, while generous, was surely not enough to tempt someone to murder.

After she had told him everything else from her discussion with Bryce, she knew there was one last thing she had to bring up. She took a big breath. "Mac, there's one more thing. It's a personal thing." She paused and then continued when she did not get a response. "He tells me you are prone to go from one girlfriend to another with no warning. I can't help but wonder...how many other women have you asked to marry you?"

Mac chuckled. "Bryce loves to needle me. You shouldn't take him too seriously. Although it's true, I have dated others since my wife passed away. I can't deny that. But I don't get serious with them and then just throw them to the wind. Most were dates that didn't go beyond two or three times out together. I didn't feel any of them would be compatible with me. I'm sure they felt the same way since none came looking for me later – these were mutual partings. Until you came along, I had never found anyone as good as my wife. I love you, Brenda Sheffield, and you only. You have nothing to worry about. I am committed to you."

As expected, his voice soothed her heart and he once again proved to be the thoughtful, caring person she knew him to be. When they hung up, she looked forward to their time together later that night. Not just fireworks and revelry, but time with Mac, the man of her dreams.

Later that afternoon, Mac called to ask Brenda if she could come down to the station before the evening festivities for some casework. "Captain Pratt is on his way down here. I'd like to get your take on what he has to say, if you have time?"

Brenda was more than happy to get the case moving along. She arrived at the police station just as Pratt pulled in. He appeared distraught as he approached the door to the building and she could see that the horrible reality of his friend's murder had sunk in.

"I know how upset you must be, Captain Pratt. I'm so sorry you have to go through losing such a good friend." He nodded and thanked her numbly. Opening the door, he allowed Brenda to precede him. She went directly to Mac's office and Pratt sat down as instructed by the clerk at the front desk.

"Captain Pratt is out there now. He seems upset. I hope he can shed some light on this mystery." Mac agreed with her and buzzed the clerk to escort Pratt into the first interrogation room. Brenda and Mac then joined him and expressed their condolences for the loss of his friend. Both were surprised at the first words that came from his mouth.

"I am sick with regret, Detective Rivers. I regret that I didn't help Bryce Jones when the boat was struggling."

At first the other two said nothing. Pratt sat calmly but deeply sad in his chair across the table. Brenda couldn't think of appropriate words to reply. Apparently, Mac was in the same position until he recovered.

"You won the race," said Mac. "I would think you would be happy with all that money. You knew the race officials had a rescue boat ready just in case, too. But no one can deny that fifty thousand dollars is quite a prize."

Pratt threw open his hands in despair. "I don't care about the money. I don't even want it any longer. I'm thinking about donating it all to charity or giving it to someone who is sincerely in need of it."

Brenda remained speechless. His words struck her as slightly odd. So far, he had not mentioned the recent murder of his good friend or the loss of the boat. Another factor hit her as strange, too. He did not meet her eyes or Mac's. Brenda wondered if Captain Pratt should be at the top of her list of suspects or if he was simply sunk too deep in mourning to look up at them.

Mac exchanged a quick glance with Brenda and then resumed the interrogation. "I find it interesting that you sped ahead of the pending disaster to win the prize and now you want to give it all up. Why is that?"

Pratt's stricken face finally lifted, though his eyes remained averted. "I did want to win. I can't deny that. We had all bet with one another that each would win. I knew from the beginning that I was a better captain than the other two were. I'm not saying they weren't expert. I'm just saying I have always been better."

"So why the regret?" Brenda waited for his answer. When he said nothing, she continued. "I'm sure the races would have begun again if all the competitors had stopped until the situation was taken care of. Everyone would have understood that under the circumstances."

He shook his head and then leaned forward. His hands wrapped his face. Perspiration emerged on his forehead between rough fingers. He sat up straight again and wiped his brow with a handkerchief. "I have more regrets than you can imagine about the whole incident. I'm relieved that young Bryce was not injured or killed out there. Yes, I wish I had done as you say, but I didn't. I wanted to win, but not like this. Eddy is gone. And I don't want the money. I don't even want the coveted silver cup. Scully should have the cup for his heroic and selfless actions."

Brenda silently agreed with that part. Mac asked Pratt if Captain Eddy had any known enemies. The captain stated he knew of no one with a grudge against the man. When pressed again, he repeated his assessment. "I can't imagine anyone not liking Captain Eddy. He was a good man and a man of honor."

He was told he was free to go but to not leave town. He rose wearily and shuffled out of the interrogation room when an officer came to lead him back to the lobby. After the door closed, Mac and Brenda discussed their take on Captain Pratt and his many regrets and few answers.

"I think he's grieving for his friend. That could explain some of the strangeness. But then again..." Brenda trailed off. Neither she nor Mac wanted to acknowledge how little they actually had to go on.

"I guess we'd better gear up for Scully next," said Mac.

chapter six

W hen Captain Scully was ushered in, his eyes were sunken and the former blustery, joking persona had left him. He sat down across from Mac and Brenda and looked directly at each of them in turn.

"I will never enter another boat race the rest of my life," he said. Solemnity had replaced his familiar joviality, and it was jarring to see him this way.

"I am so sorry for the loss of your friend and fellow captain. I know you've been racing for a long time together. How many races have you won?" Brenda asked.

"I've won a total of five in the past. Two were won right here on the Sweetfern Harbor waters. That's enough for me."

Brenda recalled Pratt's quiet boast about his racing prowess, and regretted not asking him the same question to compare to Scully's wins. Perhaps Pratt wasn't as good as he thought.

"I have questions about the incident during the race," Mac said. "When you reached the Eddy, what did you see first?"

He explained how he had focused on rescuing Bryce and paid little attention to the boat itself. "The boat was nearly down by the time I got to him. It went down faster than I would have thought possible." He paused, thinking back.

"You'd think it would be easy to figure out a boat, but so many things can go wrong. I wondered later if something came loose that caused it to take on water so quickly. It was one of the finest boats Wally Doyle ever built, in my estimation, and remember he built three identical boats for Pratt and Eddy and myself. But perhaps he got careless with a detail on that boat. I don't mean he did anything on purpose. I think something was not installed tightly enough...perhaps by mistake."

"From what I've heard of Wally, he has a stellar reputation as a shipwright. Do you really think he would make such a mistake?" Brenda pressed.

"He has a crew. They're good guys, but...I suppose it could have been one of the crew who made the mistake..." Scully trailed off, thinking, then shook his head disagreeing with himself. "No, even if a worker made a mistake, Wally examines every boat he makes with a fine-toothed comb. He would have found it and taken care of it."

Mac asked him if he knew of anyone at all who would have had a grudge against Captain Eddy. Scully replied that he couldn't think of anyone who did not like him. The man was in a sorrowful, shaken state, and Brenda thought it was hard to read his true expressions. He was given the same instructions not to leave town that Captain Pratt received.

When the door closed, Mac said to Brenda "Well, that seems like another dead end. I mean, we definitely need to question Wally and his crew, but Scully's not on the top of my list after that. Bryce is next. He's not too happy about coming in to be interrogated but I'm following protocol." Brenda could tell Mac dreaded this next interview. She realized she had no good excuse to leave before it happened, as they still had hours to go before their fireworks date that night.

"He told me earlier that he expected to be questioned. He's a detective himself, so he shouldn't be so upset about it all. And you're right when you say he should understand why he's a person of interest when he was on the boat that was the crime scene." She looked over her notes briefly as Mac got up to look through the small window in the door to see if Bryce had arrived yet.

"I have a theory about my old friend Bryce, Brenda. I think his captainship wasn't just about racing the boat. I think he wanted to be on the inside looking at clues instead of on the outside. I can't let him do that because of his ties with the race. Chief Ingram agrees with me and advised me not to include him in the investigation." Brenda finally told him to stop over-analyzing it all. Bryce should be interrogated just like anyone else and Mac didn't have to create elaborate theories to justify that. Mac stopped short of his retort to Brenda on this point when he caught a glimpse of Bryce coming down the hall toward the interrogation room. He sat back down at the table next to Brenda as Bryce walked in.

Detective Bryce Jones' face was clouded as if a storm was pending. He sat down and Mac shifted back in his chair.

"I know you aren't happy to be on that side of the table, Bryce, but you were involved in the boat race. I hope you understand."

Bryce gave a half-smile. "I know you're doing your job, Mac. I'll try to do my best. I almost drowned out there, you know. I may not look shaken up but I was awake most of the night after it all happened. That kind of thing...it changes you a little," he finished, looking away.

"I understand that," said Mac, "and I'm sincerely happy you were safely rescued before the boat went down. You were in a dangerous situation out on those waters and could have been pulled under if you tried to swim away." The detective moved forward in his chair. "The first question I have is not about the boat accident, however. I need to know why you were so anxious to get onto Eddy's boat while we were searching for clues?"

"I was told by David Williams that he was sure the race

would go forward as planned and on time. I happily volunteered to take Eddy's place – Mac, you know I've always wanted to race a sailboat – and he told me to look the boat over to get a good feel of it before the race."

Bryce said this casually, but Brenda saw that his and Mac's eyes were locked. Mac said evenly, "I know you understand how important it is that no one should intrude on a crime scene until the forensic investigation is completed." Bryce nodded. "Now that the boat is at the bottom of the ocean, we have very little evidence to go on. As a fellow detective, I'm surprised you didn't insist on delaying the race so we could get the work done."

"I had nothing to do with that decision. Frankly, that small of a crime scene would not have taken so long in my department in Brooklyn. I still don't know what was taking you so long." As he said this, Brenda could see Mac's jaw clench with suppressed anger. "But also, I was not part of the investigation, as you made very clear to me. It was David and the race officials who went to the judge to get the order. I too was surprised the judge ruled so quickly."

Mac let the silence after Bryce's words stretch out a little bit until it was uncomfortable. Then, he continued.

"Why do you think the boat sank?"

"I have no idea. Like I told Brenda, I saw a little water coming in, but I thought it was from normal waves hitting the side of the boat during the race, or from the cops who were walking on and off the boat during the investigation. Suddenly, it started coming in really fast and that's when I knew I was in trouble and radioed for help."

Brenda noticed that his recounting of the water coming in, just like when they had spoken in the library, was quick and without many details. She had to wonder if that was normal for someone who had survived a disastrous sinking, or if he was skipping over details on purpose. Since they had no way to know, they would have to continue to treat him as innocent and just hope that he tripped up, if he truly had something to hide.

"Have you overheard anyone in town speaking about the matter? I mean in a way that may shed light on who did it?"

"If I had picked up on anything, Mac, I would be right in here to tell you. I've heard nothing unusual. People are in mourning for a local hero. Captain Pratt has been taking a lot of walks along the beach according to some talk around town, both he and Scully have taken it pretty hard."

Mac excused him after Bryce stated in conclusion that he couldn't imagine who would have murdered the captain. After all, he had been living in Brooklyn for years and did not visit Sweetfern Harbor very often anymore. On his way out, he winked at Brenda and lingered in the doorway for a moment.

"I sure wish I had won that loot," he said with a smile that could have charmed a nun. "If I had, I would have showered you with anything your heart desired. We could have gone out on the town together." He ducked into the hall and disappeared just as Mac Rivers made a sound behind her that was easy to read.

When Brenda closed the door behind him, Mac spoke, ignoring the flirtatious behavior he had just witnessed. "I wonder about his statements in regard to not knowing how the boat sank. Something is not sitting right with me about Bryce Jones."

"He seems sincere when he says he has no idea how it sank, even though he doesn't have very many details about how it happened. But Mac, if Bryce had anything to do with the sinking, why would he have put himself out on the water like that?"

Mac crossed his arms over his chest and mused for a moment. "Maybe he thought the leak would be a slow one. He would win the race and the boat would sink at the finish line, or later that night. He was quite a distance ahead of the other two until he started taking on water so quickly."

Brenda still felt there was a missing piece. "How would he have known about the leak, but not how fast it would happen? Do you think he was working with someone else? Do you think he could hide something that big?"

"I don't have an answer for that, Brenda. It's just that something isn't right when it comes to Bryce and his flawless manner of getting to captain that boat at the last minute like that. Wally Doyle will be here in about forty-five minutes. Let's go grab a bite to eat and take a break."

Brenda agreed and they walked down Main Street to Morning Sun Coffee. Most of the tourist crowd had thinned out. Molly was busy with a customer and waved at them when they entered. They sat down and ordered chicken salad sandwiches and lemonade. Mac changed his drink to coffee at the last minute and the server made the notation. He rubbed at his eyes tiredly as they sat down with their food and drinks.

"Whoever killed Eddy," said Mac, "meant for the evidence to be lost. It must have been someone who knows boats well." He took a grateful sip of his coffee and seemed a little more revived.

"I agree with that. Someone who knew how to sabotage a boat without an explosion of some sort. Or at least we have to assume so, unless divers can salvage anything from the bottom of the harbor."

Mac grimaced. "The Chief found out that we have to get a special crew to come in because of how deep the harbor is at that spot. The state's diving crew was working another job up the coast so it might take them a couple more days to get the marine salvage operation going. I'm not even convinced we'll find anything in that wreck, anyway. But ignoring the boat for a minute, how did the murderer come and go unseen on Captain Eddy's boat at the harbor?"

"It tells me he was someone familiar around the harbor," Brenda said, setting down her half-eaten sandwich. "If he was familiar to those down there, he wouldn't have been noticed as a stranger in the area. Aside from the captains and the race officials, we have the boat building crew. I wonder what would be some of the reasons for a boat to sink."

"That's something to ask Wally when he comes in. I guess we'd better get back to work. Are you finished?" Brenda stated she was ready. They returned to the police station and were just getting set up in the interrogation room again when a police officer poked his head in the door and let them know that the boatwright had arrived.

The fifty-two-year-old man was shown down the hallway of the police station. Wally Doyle's physique was fit and solidly muscled, revealing the hardy work of his lifelong trade. His salt and pepper hair was thick and wavy. Dark eyebrows and deep-set brown eyes emphasized his tanned face. He greeted Brenda and Mac in a friendly tone and sat down across from them.

Brenda and Mac thanked him for coming in and extended their sympathies for the loss of his friend Captain Eddy. Brenda could see from Wally's expressive eyes that he, too, had been hard hit by Eddy's death. "Everyone in town is well-acquainted with your skills in boat building, Wally," Mac said. "But Brenda is new to town, so perhaps she doesn't know." The men's eyes swiveled to Brenda.

"That's true. Have you been at your trade long?" she asked.

Wally chuckled and nodded. "I've been building boats since I was around fifteen years old. Of course, I didn't start out actually building them, but my father taught me the basic skills from that age. I started as an apprentice and worked my way up to become a master woodworker and shipwright. I still work in the workshop near the harbor that I inherited from my father after his death. The work is something I never get tired of doing and I like to think my skills improve with every boat I build."

Brenda commented on the beauty of Captain Eddy's boat. "It was the first of the three we had time to tour. As you know, we found his body that morning and so that halted everything."

Wally's eyes grew serious. "It was bad enough the boat was destroyed, but worse that someone killed one of the finest seamen I've ever known. Eddy was well liked and he knew what he was doing out on the waters. I can't imagine who would have wanted him dead."

"I have questions regarding the boat itself," Mac said. "Do you have any idea why the boat would have sunk?"

Wally shook his head slowly as if still in shock one of his boats ended in such a disastrous manner. "I won't know what happened unless the boat can be brought up from the harbor. I checked each of those boats thoroughly just a few hours before it was time for the race. I believe it was around eight in the morning. I would have to look in my records to get the exact time. I had to sign off on an inspection sheet for the race officials. Everything was perfect and the boats were ready."

"How friendly were you with Captain Eddy?" asked Mac.

"I knew all three of the captains quite well from working closely together on ship repairs over the years and building these new boats. We were all excited about the race. They were in their element and us seamen love nothing more than a friendly ear who will listen to us go on about our ships," he said fondly and a little bit sadly. "We all looked forward to the competition. It's the biggest event in Sweetfern Harbor in the summertime."

"Did any one of the three indicate trouble ahead?" Brenda asked. Wally asked for clarification. "I mean did any of them say something that might have told you things might be amiss? Perhaps facial expressions were different or maybe one of them said something that was out of context?"

Wally shook his head. "There was nothing different from any other year. Scully and Pratt ribbed each other as usual about their certainty of winning. Eddy chimed in a little but his mannerisms never spilled over like the other two. Eddy was always quieter and he was a thinker more than outwardly carrying on like Scully and Pratt. He had a few wins under his belt, too. They often raced away from Sweetfern Harbor, but no races equaled the popularity this one holds." He paused. "In answer to your question, everything seemed as normal as usual before a big race like this one."

"If they're able to bring the boat up," Mac said, "it will be a while before you can go over it to see what caused it to sink."

Wally said he understood. "I just want to know what happened. I can say for sure that the boat was in top shape before the race."

After he was excused, Mac invited Brenda back to his office where they discussed Wally Doyle and went over their notes.

"I'm going to go back down to the harbor as soon as possible. I want to ask some of the business owners along the harbor if they saw Wally and the captains together earlier that day."

Brenda agreed it was a good idea. "We didn't see any of them down there that morning since they were all at Morning Sun by the time we toured." She picked up a pen on Mac's desk and tapped it lightly on his desk. "I don't think Wally had anything to do with Eddy's murder. But we should still talk to his crew of workers, just in case."

Mac wanted to play Devil's Advocate about Wally's possible involvement, but in the end, he brushed over that idea when they heard David Williams' voice from the front. Brenda glanced at the clock and saw that they still had plenty of time for another interview. When the clerk buzzed Mac's office, he told her to take the race official to the same interrogation room as before.

"I've asked Brenda to sit in on the interrogations," Mac said as they entered and sat down across from the race official. David indicated he had no problem with that.

"I know what you did with the case of Ellen Teague's murder. I'm anxious to get to the bottom of this one, too, like the rest of the town," said David.

Mac asked him where he had been in the time frame already established. David told them he was down on the docks with his fellow race officials. As an anchor on the local news, David was not only calling the race, but acting as the on-air race commentator for the live broadcast of the sailboat race. "I had the cameraman with me. We were filming everything that had to do with the race. I was due to go live. As the head race official, I had to monitor the whole race and pronounce the winner at the end, of course."

"Did you go onto the boats or just film close up?" Brenda asked.

"To tell you the truth, water is not my thing...I was raised close to the ocean and I did learn to swim as a child, but it's been a long time since I've enjoyed being in the water. I did go onto Scully's boat since it was expected of me if I wanted to tell the story of the race. I have to admit my legs wobbled a little."

"Where does that fear come from?" Brenda asked, curious to see this fear in an otherwise confident man.

He rolled his eyes a little at himself and then settled in. "I may as well tell you the story. Most people around here recall it like it happened yesterday. As a kid, I was fascinated with boats. Until I was a teenager the water was my heaven on earth. Then one day several of us skipped school to take a sailboat out. It belonged to my best friend's father. While we were on the water, a storm came up and I was washed overboard. Things flew from the boat and a small cooler flipped out and hit me on the head. I was partially knocked out but not enough that I didn't know I was drowning. It seemed hours before I was rescued by one of the boys. They thought it was funny. What do teenagers know about head injuries? Two of them pulled me in but it left a deep scar of fear in me."

"So ever since then, you lost your love of boats?" Brenda watched his eyes.

"I remain fascinated with boats of all kinds. It's the water I fear. I've never been out on the water since that incident." He seemed distracted and changed the subject. "I'm sorry, Mac, about how aggressive I was in getting the court order to go forward with the race. I regret it now but I got caught up in the momentum of the crowd and the race itself. You have no idea what kind of pressure we were under financially when we realized how much we would owe the crowd in refunds. The race fund would probably go bankrupt and my fellow race officials and I realized that this might be the last year ever for the race, if that happened."

"What's done is done," said Mac. "I'm more concerned now that the evidence has been washed away. I knew the crime scene would be contaminated during the race, but when the boat sank, I knew we would have very little to go on, even if we could raise the boat." Even though his voice was calm, Brenda sensed that Mac remained upset with David and the judge. She couldn't blame him. This case was frustrating enough without losing evidence that could point to the killer. "I'll have to check on your alibi, David. The fact that you were filming will be in your favor." He told David he was free to go.

As Mac shuffled his notes into a pile, Brenda watched David leave with a sinking feeling that these interviews were not generating the leads that they needed. They would have to find another way to crack the case.

chapter seven

Mac and Brenda walked back to his office. "Let's go talk with Allie about her dad's alibi," said Brenda. "Then we can stop by Sweet Treats and talk with Hope. I don't know David all that well except for what I've seen of him on television. I'd like to see a more personal side of him."

"I think he's a good guy all around, but he's not a personable person in public. Except in front of an audience, of course."

When they arrived at the bed and breakfast they went into Allie's small office behind the front desk. She was on the phone booking a reservation. When she finished, she smiled at the two of them expectantly. Brenda sat down in one of the narrow wingback chairs and Mac took the other one.

"We just spoke with your dad, Allie," Brenda said. "Do you know what he was doing the morning of the race?"

Allie's eyes widened. "Is he a suspect?"

"No, he isn't. We're just verifying everyone's whereabouts."

"We're doing this with everyone connected with the boat race first," Mac added.

"He was on TV," said Allie. "I know he was filming down

at the harbor side at first, because that's where he said he was meeting the camera crew when he left early that morning. And then his crew followed him to the stands where the race began. I know he did that because in between my work here I watched him." She gestured toward the twenty-inch television in the corner of the office that was often tuned to her father's local channel.

"Before he went to the viewing platform, did he go out on the water to show how one of the boats runs?" Mac asked. "I mean, did he go out with one of the captains, maybe take a quick ride around the harbor?"

"I'm sure he didn't do that," said Allie. Her tone emphasized her words with a look of finality. "He's not at all comfortable going out on water. Something happened to him a long time ago when he was a teenager and he doesn't like water or watersports of any kind since then."

They stood to go and thanked David's daughter for her input. Brenda was relieved that Allie was able to back up her father's answers, because it would have been very tense at the Sheffield Bed and Breakfast if her own receptionist's father were to be a main suspect. She and Mac climbed into Mac's car and drove down to Sweet Treats. The aroma of pastries filled their nostrils in the bakery and David's wife waved them in. "I'll get the rolls from the oven and be right with you."

Brenda turned to Mac with eyes wide. "I won't be able to resist one of those cinnamon rolls. How about you?"

"This place is too tempting," he agreed, looking around at the displays of baked goods and specialty cakes. They eagerly walked up to the counter.

Hope returned and took their orders. She called to her helper from the back and asked her to take over in front while she talked with the detective and Brenda. They carried rolls and coffee to a small table at the end of the shop and Hope pulled up a chair for herself. Mac asked her the same questions Allie had answered. Although she too was worried at first that her husband might be a suspect, after they reassured her it was a routine alibi check, Hope's answers matched her daughter's.

"Can you think of anyone who may have had a grudge against Captain Eddy? I know you had quite a crowd of customers during the weekend. I'm wondering if you overheard anyone speak ill of him."

"It was a busy time in here but I only heard everyone talk about how much they looked forward to the big weekend. I didn't hear anything said maliciously against any of the three captains. There were playful arguments about who would win, but nothing seriously negative." She looked intently at the two in front of her. "I know everyone involved in the race is suspect at this point, but I can assure you David would never hurt a fly, much less kill someone like Captain Eddy. He liked the man so much. David told me Eddy always made the world a better place." They finished off their cinnamon rolls and coffee, chatting with Hope a little bit more, but there was nothing more to hear that would help them.

Outside Sweet Treats, Mac turned to Brenda. "I'll pick you up in time for the fireworks," he said a little tiredly.

"I look forward to tonight, Mac," said Brenda, her eyes searching his. She silently hoped he wouldn't be too distracted by the investigation to enjoy the night of celebrations. Brenda knew him well enough to understand that he would continue working the case in spite of the fireworks shooting off. They parted ways, with Mac giving her a brief kiss on the cheek. She held tight to the warmth of that kiss as she walked herself home to get ready for their evening together.

That evening, Mac looked considerably more refreshed, having taken a shower and changed into a crisp linen shirt that showed off his broad shoulders. When he took Brenda's hand and they walked toward the harbor, she enjoyed the fresh scent of his cologne and was glad she had chosen to change into a light, flowing summer dress. But despite the prospect of an entertaining evening ahead, they were both lost in thought about the case. Mac spoke first.

"I've found no evidence of a murder suspect from the information I have at the station. If I could find a motive for it, I could have a lead."

"I agree it is frustrating. But I know you're doing all the right things. Something will turn up soon."

Mac's hand grew warmer as he squeezed hers a little, grateful for the reassurance. "It may have been one of the hundreds of tourists in town. Maybe someone who knew Eddy before he ever arrived here did it."

"If it was a tourist," said Brenda unhappily, "the culprit could have left town by now."

They didn't speak for a few minutes, thinking about the possibilities. Searching for and bringing in every tourist for questioning was impossible. Not to mention the troublesome fact that no strangers had been seen coming and going on the docks that night or that morning after Mac had questioned the business owners along the docks where the sailboats had been moored.

"Let's try to enjoy the spectacle tonight. Of course, we'll need to be aware of conversations and mannerisms, especially of anyone talking about the crime," Mac said. "It will be a while before gossip tones down around here. I just hope we can get to the bottom of it all."

They settled near the top of the grassy bank that overlooked the ocean. A small cruiser with fireworks was anchored yards away from the shore and as the twilight deepened around them into night, the exhibition finally started. Among the oohs and ahhs of the crowd, Brenda picked up a comment here and there speculating about who killed the captain. Those observations surfaced when Captain Scully turned and waved to the crowd before sitting down in one of the lawn chairs set aside in a special section for race entrants and officials. Brenda searched in the dim light for Captain Pratt. Mac started to wonder where the man was, too, but just then Captain Pratt arrived and sat next to Scully. The crowd roared when the fireworks shot higher and higher into the air, bursting in a way that seemed to cover the onlookers while reflecting on the water in dazzling effects. Brenda had never seen anything like it. After forty-five minutes, the finale of the display exploded in a triumph of color and the crowd clapped and cheered. Then the spectators began to disperse under the drifting haze that settled beneath the starry night sky.

Brenda looked at the captains. Scully scribbled his autograph on various papers thrust at him from the onlookers. Captain Pratt was nowhere to be seen. She mentioned this to Mac who pointed to the edge of the water. Captain Pratt stood in the sand and looked out onto the ocean. He turned around and started to leave when fans approached him. He smiled patiently and then signed his name again and again. As she and Mac stood watching from their hill, they saw Pratt finally leave and Brenda presumed he was headed back to his boat for some peace and quiet. He seemed somber and she thought he must be seeking some time alone.

"I'm ready for a cold drink," said Mac. Brenda agreed and together they walked along the boardwalk where vendors had set up stalls selling food and drink. Jenny and Phyllis were in front of them and William tagged behind the two women. They all chatted about the fireworks display.

"I could have watched it all night long," said Phyllis. They found a picnic table and all sat and enjoyed their refreshments, savoring the festive atmosphere and chatting. Brenda looked around but there were few people nearby, so she couldn't listen in on the conversations of the crowd as much as she wished she could.

At last, Brenda felt tiredness overtake her, so she stood up and Mac did the same. "I'm ready to turn in for the night," she said with a yawn.

Phyllis and William stated they were going to walk around a while longer and headed off toward the harbor side. When Mac offered to walk Brenda home, she protested until Jenny finally stepped in and convinced her father to come home and get some rest. Both Jenny and Brenda could plainly see that Mac was fatigued, though he was reluctant to admit it. He finally agreed and kissed Brenda lightly when she insisted she would be fine walking alone to the bed and breakfast.

"I'll enjoy the short walk back and will see you sometime tomorrow." She waved goodbye as Mac and his daughter climbed into Jenny's car and drove away.

When she started up the driveway to the bed and breakfast, she smiled. The windows of Sheffield House shone out into the dark summer night. The lights were inviting and she watched a few guests enter ahead of her. Someone sat on the steps of the front veranda. The form was quite large, which soothed her initial fear – she wouldn't have to face Bryce Jones tonight. As she drew closer, she realized it was Captain Pratt. In his right hand, he clutched a small cardboard box.

"Good evening, Captain Pratt. You're out late tonight. What brings you to the Sheffield Bed and Breakfast?"

He attempted a smile. "I hoped you had not gone to bed. I've been waiting to talk with you." He shuffled to his feet with the box in his hand. "I know it's late but I hope you can spare a few minutes."

She was dying of curiosity and assured him she had time. They walked up the steps and sat on the porch swing.

"I guess you're wondering what's in this cardboard box,"

Pratt said. "I have photos I want to show you that Eddy and I took just a week ago. It's still hard to believe he's gone." In the moonlight Brenda could see his eyes misted when he said that.

"Me, too. I am curious to see the pictures."

"They're from a day when we went out on my boat to do some fishing." Brenda held her breath. Captain Pratt was finally opening up. Was this going to be the clue or confession that cracked the case of Captain Eddy's murder? "I'm telling you this because I want to help solve this case. Captain Eddy was a brother to me, but he meant more than that to me. He was the best man I've ever known." He opened the lid and took out the first picture and held it up for her proudly. "Look at this one. This is when Eddy caught the biggest fish I've ever seen. He threw it back. When I asked him why he did that, he said if the fish had lived this long he deserved to finish his life in the sea. I look at that as symbolic in a way...he was good-hearted like that. Though unlike that fish, poor Eddy didn't die in the sea he loved, did he?"

"No, he didn't."

Pratt handed her the box mutely and Brenda thumbed through the pictures one by one. Mixed in with the recent pictures were a few other photos that showed the captains and friends fishing, sailing, and boating together in happier times. Photos of their catches with pride beaming on their faces, or the three captains posing together showing off a custom flag embroidered with their names above an anchor to symbolize their friendship. They clearly loved fishing, as some of the pictures were crowded with the rods and all the paraphernalia that went along with the sport.

"Some of these pictures show the inside of my boat," Pratt said. "I was proud of the craftsmanship Wally demonstrated when he built the boat. It was every inch a beauty. This is the engine compartment."

Brenda held the photo in her hand. "Let's go inside so I

can get a better look. The porch light doesn't do justice to these pictures."

They moved inside and Brenda looked closely at the engine and its complicated machinery that shone with brass fittings and complex dials. "This engine looks new."

"When we were on the water fishing one day a couple weeks ago, just after the boats were finished, my engine malfunctioned. I knew that wouldn't be a good thing in a race that I meant to win. So I went to Wally Doyle and he replaced it with this new one."

"Did he say why it malfunctioned? Why replace it and not just repair it?"

"He didn't say and I didn't ask. The new one was worth taking a picture of after he replaced the bad one. I wanted to show it off to the other two. Scully and Eddy were impressed. It was a state-of-the-art engine and I think they were a little jealous." He laughed. "Their engines were just as good, but this one was a newer model and built to last a much longer time, probably longer than the boat would. It had the same power as theirs did, however. Wally made sure to keep the playing field even between us when it came to building the boats."

Brenda held the photo. Thoughts raced through her mind. "I know it's late, Captain Pratt, but do you mind if we go down to look at your boat?"

Excitement filled Pratt's eyes. "If you think it's important I'm happy to give you a tour. It's a mighty fine boat and I'm proud to show it off."

"Let's drive down there since it's so late. We can go in my car." Pratt agreed to let her drive them down there. The night was getting late and though some revelers were still out, the crowds had thinned and they easily passed through the busier Main Street district to get to the parking lot near the docks.

When they got to the boat, Pratt started expounding on

the qualities of the wood and the other amenities in the boat. Brenda could tell he was ready to natter on for quite a while, so she interrupted him politely, smiling.

"Did you mean it when you said you wanted to help solve the crime?"

"Of course. Tell me what you need from me."

She told him she wished to inspect the engine. "I'd like to see it firsthand."

Pride flushed in Pratt's face. He took her down into the cabin and back to the engine compartment which he opened with a flourish. Then he stopped in his tracks. He leaned over and examined the machinery from all sides.

"I just wanted to make sure this is the new engine...and it is. It's the one Wally Doyle put in here after the other one malfunctioned."

"Are you sure of that?"

"I know for certain it's the same engine. Believe me when I say I recognize the state-of-the-art one he put in here." He nodded his head vigorously. "It's definitely the same engine." He gazed upon it with pride once more and stepped back to let her look more closely. Try as she might, she could not see anything out of place.

Brenda walked ahead of Captain Pratt back up the stairs. She pointed to the cotton curtains. "Who made the curtains? They appear handmade."

Captain Pratt told her of the seamstress hired by Wally Doyle for shipboard work. "She's worked for him for a long time. She's quite the expert, don't you think? Always does a fine—" He took a second look. Then he fingered the material and spread it across his hand. "This isn't the original pattern he had her put in here."

Brenda stopped on the stair and turned back to come closer. "How can you tell?"

"I chose the sailboat pattern. It was intricate like this, but it was sailboats and not yachts. Eddy wanted the yachts because that was his dream. He told me more than once that when he quit racing boats he would buy a yacht and cruise the waters until he died. I can't believe that Wally would have made this mistake...I know for certain I had the sailboat pattern because I showed it off so many times when folks came around for tours." He stared at the fabric in consternation.

"Look around some more," Brenda said, trying to suppress her suspicions. "Is anything else out of place or different?" She began to wonder if Pratt was showing her his boat or someone else's. "You're sure this is your boat and not Scully's?"

He looked hard at her. "I know my boat when I see it. Scully's is right over there where it always is. This is where I always dock mine. This is my boat." He scratched his head. "I'm sorry. There is something mysterious about it all. I'm sure it's my boat but I feel I may be going crazy after seeing those curtains. Ah, but look at these scuff marks. I always get scuff marks right away, I'm a heavy-heeled man..." He knelt down to take a closer look. He was curiously silent, tracing the black streaks of a boot heel on the floor. Brenda looked at Pratt's own boots and could see they were more of a reddish-brown rubber. Finally, he stood up, a look of consternation on his face. "These don't match any of my shoes. They are a different brand."

She looked around, her mind racing. "I see you like a few sea knick-knacks in your kitchen."

Now Pratt was aghast, turning to look. "What? No—Eddy liked that stuff. I never liked that bric-a-brac clutter like he did. I don't get it. This doesn't look like my boat the more I look around. I haven't walked through it like this since the race." The man was clearly befuddled by this and kept turning around as if he would find a clue that would correct the strangeness of what he saw before him.

Brenda started to walk outside onto the deck. She saw

Scully's boat where it should be. She walked around to the front of the boat and looked closely at the name painted on the vessel. It read *Pratt* but something was amiss, even in the dim evening light.

"It's my boat all right," said Captain Pratt coming up behind her. "It says so right there."

"Take a closer look. Your name has been painted over someone else's." She pointed out the rough edges of the paint around his name that were just barely visible up close in the lights from the harbor side street lamps. "I'm convinced this is actually Captain Eddy's boat and not yours." Even though it was getting very late, she quickly dialed Mac and told him to come as soon as possible to the harbor. "Come to Captain Pratt's boat."

She looked at Pratt when she ended the call. His face was ashen. "So someone switched things around." Brenda nodded in agreement.

"I'd like for you to give me any and all photos you have of your boat. I think we can assume it is the one that sank the day of the race and is a crime scene at the bottom of the ocean."

"I have plenty besides the ones we have here. I'll get them to you." He stopped talking. Then he spoke softly. "Well, no. Most of the photos went down with my boat, if you're correct. But I have some in my suitcase that is stored in the harbor master's office. I'll get them."

While he did that, Brenda met Mac Rivers who hurried along the dock. Brenda told him everything she knew and his eyes widened as he stepped back to view the boat beside them in a whole new light.

chapter eight

A s Brenda finished telling him everything she had learned from Pratt, Mac sensed the excitement in her demeanor. He smiled briefly to see her so excited to help move the investigation forward, and he, too, felt relief at this new development.

"I don't think Pratt had anything to do with it, but someone went to a lot of trouble switching the boats." She showed Mac the painted-over name on the boat they approached. "Pratt is looking for more photos of his boat that sank."

"Wally's identical boats made it hard to see the difference. I'm surprised Pratt didn't notice before now," Mac said, shining his flashlight on the boat.

"He said he hadn't been on the boat much since the race. There was nothing to make him think it wasn't his." At his questions, Brenda explained how she found Captain Pratt on her doorstep after walking home. "When I saw the picture of his new engine I had an idea to come down with him to look at it, just in case. He swears it's the same engine Wally put in after his malfunctioned on a fishing trip. But this definitely isn't his boat." She explained to Mac how confused Pratt had been when he discovered the switch, which led her to believe he genuinely had no idea it had happened until now.

"Whoever went to the trouble of painting over Eddy's name could have also had time to switch the engines. What if they put the malfunctioning engine in the sailboat that sunk? We need to know who had access to where the malfunctioning engine was stored," Mac said firmly.

Brenda agreed. "Wally might think he knows where the old one is. But right now, it's down with the sunken boat. We definitely need to question him and his work crew in the morning."

Mac put a call in to Chief Bob Ingram and told him of the discovery. Despite the late hour, the Chief stated he was on his way to the harbor. Captain Pratt rejoined them on the deck and showed them the few pictures he had of his boat.

"This is my boat...my real boat, which I now know is beneath the water." He showed them a few pictures of the cabin and the kitchen which, in contrast to the decorations Brenda had just seen inside, was quite different – tidy and spartan. The sailboat pattern on the curtains was also plainly visible in several of the photos. As he flipped through the small stack of photos he had found, there was one showing the deck of a boat.

"What did you keep this wooden barrel on the deck for?" Mac asked, pointing out a detail.

"I always kept a large wooden vat of some kind on deck. This one isn't mine. I know it's Eddy's. He did the same as I did. We both liked to race boats but we like to fish more. It was handy to throw the fish in when we fished from the deck." His eyes grew sad. "It's hard for me to think about someone shoving Eddy's head into it to cause his death. Who would have done something like that?"

"We don't know that answer," Brenda said apologetically, "but we're working on it. Do you happen to have a receipt showing the new engine?"

Pratt opened his hands wide. "Not with me. That's something else that's at the bottom of the ocean."

The police chief arrived and he asked Captain Pratt's permission to look through the boat. He, Mac and Brenda searched the boat for clues. Pratt followed them and assisted with answers and suggestions as they went through the vessel. At last they seemed satisfied.

"Don't leave the harbor with this boat," said Chief Ingram, tiredly wiping his hand across his forehead. "We'll probably be back tomorrow first thing in the morning to talk some more." He assured Pratt that it was fine for him to sleep on the boat as usual. "Don't tell anyone of our findings here tonight. That includes Captain Scully."

"I'm sure Scully had nothing to do with any of this," Pratt protested.

"It doesn't matter what anyone thinks. Right now, everyone is a suspect. Keep this information to yourself." Chief Ingram's face was stern. Captain Pratt readily agreed with his request.

They all said goodnight and Mac offered Brenda a ride home. She explained she had arrived in her own car and they said goodnight for the second time that evening. She drove home with her excitement fading into fatigue by degrees. When she glanced in her rearview mirror she saw Mac's car behind her. Back at the bed and breakfast, Brenda invited him in when she saw his car still idling in the driveway and he agreed. Neither of them were quite ready to say goodnight after all, after the excitement of the late-night discovery.

But as they walked through the dew-kissed grass toward the garden, instead of discussing the developments of the past few hours, Brenda brought up the subject of their engagement.

"The boat races are over and things are calming down around here," she said. "When is a good time to announce our engagement?" He squeezed her hand as they reached the garden bench and sat down together. He turned to look at her with a soft sigh.

"I suppose my hesitation is that I want you all to myself. Once we announce it we will be bombarded with attention. Everyone will have questions and ideas on how the wedding should play out and who knows the advice that will hit us right and left." He ducked his head down bashfully and she started to understand the fierce need for privacy that he cherished in his life.

Brenda smiled. "What you say is true. Maybe we should just enjoy it between us alone for a time. But I'm not letting you off the hook, Mac Rivers. When I think we should let the world know, that's when it will happen. You may guard your private life for a little while yet, but this engagement is mine, too. I need the support and love of my friends around me. So be prepared," she teased him.

His response was a chuckle. Brenda leaned into his shoulder for a moment, then went to the kitchen and brought a cold beer to him and a glass of wine for herself. They sat in comfortable silence for a few minutes. Neither could get their minds off the events at the harbor.

"What's your next step in regard to the switched boats?" Brenda asked.

"I think both of us should pay a visit to Wally Doyle's and his crew first thing tomorrow morning."

"He doesn't seem to be someone who would commit murder but he definitely is someone who needs to answer pertinent questions." Brenda sipped her wine. "I am finding this whole boating thing fascinating. Who knew racing boats could be so luxurious?"

"It isn't the first time I've seen one," Mac said. His eyes danced when he looked at her. "I've been around here a long time and have seen more than one boat race. Haven't you noticed some of the boats that visitors dock along the harbor?"

"I have noticed but have never been inside any of them until now. Maybe one day I'll get to visit one that isn't a crime scene!" Brenda took another drink of her wine. "Back to Wally now. I have a feeling you may be suspecting him."

"In my field, I never take it for granted that certain persons of interest aren't capable of committing a crime like that," Mac said. "I do agree that Wally doesn't seem like a murderer. He's had a spotless life when it comes to any infractions of the law and I've known him a long time. But he had opportunity. That's not much, but we do have to rule him out. Not to mention his crew."

Brenda stifled a yawn and Mac glanced at his watch. It was well past midnight and he stood to go. They walked back to the kitchen together to deposit their drinks.

"Thanks for the beer and the good company," he said. "We both need to get some sleep. We have a lot of work waiting for us." He leaned over and kissed Brenda. "I'll let myself out."

Brenda yawned again. "I apologize for not stifling that yawn. The day and the wine contributed." She followed him to the door where he kissed her, leaning in with a warmth that made her tingle.

After he left, Brenda brushed her hand softly across her lips and then locked the front door. For the first time in a long time, when she went into her apartment she didn't feel like the engagement ring was taunting her from its hiding place. It was safe and sound where it was supposed to be – just like her.

The next morning, Brenda met Mac at Jenny's Blossoms when he dropped his daughter off for work.

"When will your car be ready again?" Brenda directed her question to Jenny.

"I should have it back by the end of the day. I'm thankful

it was nothing serious, but Randy told me I'd probably need new brakes in a few months. Guess I'll have to start saving up for that next."

Jenny's long blonde hair shook a little as she laughed. Brenda couldn't recall ever seeing Jenny not upbeat and outgoing in mannerisms. She kept up with everything going on in Sweetfern Harbor, and today was no exception. She leaned in confidentially toward Brenda.

"I heard Captain Scully isn't as outgoing as he was before the races. I think the death of his good friend really shook him." She paused for a brief moment. "It didn't help that he rescued Bryce Jones just before that boat sank. That would be enough to shake me up."

"Have you been around Scully much since the races?" Brenda asked.

"He was in the coffee shop early this morning. Someone offered sympathy at the loss of his friend. He just nodded and took a drink of his latté. He isn't the same man and that's for sure." Jenny turned when she heard the back doorbell to her shop ring. "That's my delivery. I'd better go."

They wished her a good day. "And a prosperous one," said her father. They heard Jenny's melodious laugh on her way to the back door.

"Let's go see Wally now. We can walk down there," Mac said.

When they got to the shipwright's shop, Brenda was impressed at how large the workshop was. There was a large fenced area that held open-air supplies, parking for the workers, and trailers for the boats, as well as a tall warehouse that served as the main boat building facility. Mac told her the height of the building was so it could accommodate the deep keels of the sailboats Wally built. The shop was built behind a building that had originally been a house, and Wally's father had expanded it into the warehouse space and the fenced yard behind. They entered through a side door of the warehouse workshop. Several workers were busy in the back and Wally came forward. He greeted them and Mac asked if there was someplace private they could talk.

He wiped his hands on his thick canvas apron with a smile. "I expected to see you at some point. Let's go back to my office."

He escorted them to a spacious room that held a large oak desk with a computer and printer set at the end of it. Behind was a credenza, also oak. Several cushioned chairs were scattered opposite Wally's desk. As he took off his apron, he winced when he sat down, and she noticed a black nylon back brace velcroed around his trim waist. She asked him if he was okay and he waved off her concern, explaining that he had long had a bad back. "These days we have machines that do the heavy lifting for us, but when I was a younger man...let's just say my doctor wishes I hadn't showed off so much around the shop!" A small fireplace was in the far corner and two winged chairs flanked it. Brenda realized they must be in the part of the building that was part of the old house. It was cozy, with wood paneled walls and a few old paintings of seafaring ships. On one wall were mounted a number of commendations and newspaper articles written about his company and its quality craftsmanship.

Wally gestured toward the chairs across from him and asked if they wanted anything to drink. Both declined, though Brenda had the feeling anything they may ask for was at hand for visitors or prospective customers. Wally's boats were not cheap and everywhere she could see the evidence of the prosperous nature of his work.

Nevertheless, they were there about much more pressing matters. She got right to the point. "When did Eddy's and Pratt's boats get switched?" Brenda asked.

Wally's face went blank. He shook his head. "What? They

didn't get switched. There was no reason to do so. All three boats were identical except for the interior finishes. Scully didn't have a preference about most things, but Pratt and Eddy specified certain things such as the type of wood finish in the interior. They even had their own ideas about specific patterns in the kitchen curtains. I had my seamstress make them the way they wanted," he finished proudly. "So there's no way I could have switched the boats even if I tried."

"Did you replace an engine on Captain Pratt's boat?" Mac pressed.

"I did that when his engine malfunctioned out on the water one day recently. He and Captain Eddy went out fishing and weren't sure they were going to make it back to shore. The engine kept cutting out. When I took a look, I couldn't figure out what was wrong with it, so I think it came from the factory defective. I replaced it with a newer one. The company told me they now make them to last much longer than the others. Pratt was happy to show it off to the other two."

"Do you have proof that the new engine went into that particular boat?" Brenda watched his eyes. There was no hesitation.

Wally opened a drawer and pulled out a folder. "Of course. I'm still old fashioned. I have it all on my computer but I believe in hard copies. Here it is." He opened the folder that had Captain Pratt's name on it and spread the receipts in front of them. The invoice for the replaced engine was there, and so was the labor sheet showing the date and the time that Wally had replaced the engine. Everything was as Pratt had told them.

Brenda spoke. "I'd like to see the old engine you took from the boat for comparison. Do you still have it or did you discard it?"

Wally said he kept it and led them back to the workshop.

"I tried to return it to the company, but they don't make that model anymore, so they told me I could scrap it. But I thought maybe one of the guys could figure out what was wrong with it, maybe salvage a few parts..." They followed him to the shop area, where he stopped. He searched for several minutes with no result. "I know it was right here where I tagged it with the boat number and Pratt's name." He called to his workers. "Did any of you move the old engine I took from Captain Pratt's boat?"

Brenda watched each face. All spoke in the negative. One remarked they all knew better than to move things once Wally set them down. The other three laughed. Wally made the remark that they learned their lessons well. Then he turned apologetically to Mac and Brenda.

"I have no idea where it is. It's heavy so I can't imagine someone just walked off with it. I can assure you that engine was not safe. It could have caused a fire in an instant. They're lucky they made it back to shore with it the first time it died. The electrical system was off and could have bled fuel and caught the boat on fire."

"What about sinking a boat? Would a malfunctioning engine cause a boat to sink?" Brenda asked.

Wally was taken aback when she said this, clearly understanding the implication. "Not in my experience. Usually it would catch on fire, first. But if the raw-water hose ruptures and comes off a fitting in the engine, a boat would sink. Yes."

"Wouldn't that mean it would sink while docked? Before it even gets out on the water?" Mac asked.

"Not necessarily. In the case of a hose rupture, the water seeps in faster if the boat is running, since the water is running through the engine at a faster rate. Even under sailing power, when they're not using the engine much, the raw-water hose is feeding water through the engine at a pretty fast rate. The engine I took out of Pratt's boat did show wear in that hose which was another reason I had to replace it right away." He thought for a few seconds. "Now that I think about it, I doubt very much it came from the factory that way. It's almost as if someone purposely caused the slight rupture I noted." He looked around again as if hoping the engine would suddenly appear. "I have no idea where that engine is but maybe one of the guys on the other shift moved it with the forklift. When I find it I'll call you right away."

After they left the shop, Brenda spoke. "I think that old engine is underwater. Someone got into Wally's shop and took it and put it back into Captain Pratt's boat. The same person painted over Eddy's name with Pratt's name instead."

"That would mean the killer also tampered with the engine's hose and that's how it sank once on water. I don't understand why the boats were switched, or when. That part makes no sense." Mac wiped his brow with the back of his hand.

"I think we'd better get Captain Scully down for questioning," Brenda said. Mac agreed.

"Let's grab lunch at Morning Sun and something cool to drink."

Molly waved from the back of the shop and then came over to their table. "You both look like you need a cold lemonade to cool you off. It's gotten hot out there today." They agreed gratefully and she left to get their drinks.

They discussed their findings quietly. Several people sat a few tables away from them out of earshot.

"Wally seemed completely surprised at the switching of boats," said Brenda. "He seemed completely open and honest. What was your take on him?"

"I picked up the same reaction. My guess is that his second shift crew won't have any answers, either. He doesn't know where the old engine is because someone stole it from him. I'll go back soon and talk with all of his crew. I know he checks them out, but we can't be too careful."

Brenda took a sip of her lemonade and pondered just how many hands had to touch each boat before it was ready to go out on the water, and how one malevolent person had wrecked all that by taking one man's life and nearly drowning another one.

chapter nine

Brenda savored the cold lemonade. She looked toward the door of the shop to see Pete Graham walk in. Sweetfern Harbor's postal carrier wiped his brow and handed Molly her mail. Their eyes locked lovingly for a few seconds before he pulled away and greeted Mac and Brenda. He looked longingly at their lemonades. Before he could open his mouth to say hello, he saw one more glass slide onto the table in front of him. Molly smiled at him when he turned in surprise and told him she knew he needed a break.

"How's the case coming along?" he asked the detective as he took a long swig from his glass.

Mac and Brenda exchanged a quick glance. They knew better than to share too much information with Pete Graham. It seemed his mission in life was not just to carry the mail, but to carry as much gossip from shop to shop on his route as possible.

"It's coming along, but nothing concrete yet." Mac sipped his drink.

"Everyone hopes the killer is found out soon," Pete said. "I met Captain Eddy a few times. He seemed like a real nice guy. The whole town is upset he was killed that way. Poor man. I'm sure his memorial service will be packed when they hold it next week. I keep thinking about how he must have suffered fighting off his killer." Pete shook his head sadly.

The other two agreed. "The murderer will be found out. When that time comes, everyone will get the news." Brenda smiled after her statement. Pete's eyes held disappointment that he didn't get any scoops to share, but he had no choice other than to accept the news.

Mac and Brenda laughed softly together after he left. "I know he was hoping for more but he's crazy if he thinks we don't know his reputation for gossip. We can't let anything out yet," Mac said. Brenda nodded and looked at the menu when Molly approached with her notepad poised for their orders. She ordered a tossed salad and more lemonade and Mac ordered a ham salad sandwich. "I'll take more lemonade, too," he told Molly and she returned to the kitchen to prepare their orders.

"I think we should bring Bryce back in when we call Scully," Brenda said, thinking over how the new discovery of the boat switch might change everyone's perspective. Mac showed surprise and she explained her thinking. "He should see the whole picture and know why that boat sank. I'll get all the photos of Captain Pratt's boat from him. We should put them up on a sort of display board before they come in."

"Do you mean like an investigation board?" Brenda nodded yes. "We have a huge bulletin board where we sometimes pin up evidence to be studied during a crime investigation. I think it is available now or, if it isn't, we have another one in the back storeroom. I think we should include Wally, too. He can back up our findings and shed some light on this for the others." As their food arrived and they ate, they eagerly went over the details of what could be included on the board to help visualize the various components of the investigation.

Once back at the police station, Mac placed the large board

in the larger interrogation room and Brenda fetched helpful supplies like pushpins, a spare map, and some labels. Then Mac summoned Bryce, Wally and Captain Scully down to headquarters. "Be here in half an hour," he told all three.

Meanwhile, Brenda called Captain Pratt and asked him to bring the photos down to the police station right away. She wanted him there before the others so he could help get the pictures in order up on the board. He arrived a few minutes later, and they pinned them up alongside the map, which they labeled with the various locations pertinent to the investigation.

"That boat is a beauty for sure," said Brenda, stepping back to admire their handiwork. She noted how Pratt beamed at the compliment.

"Wally Doyle knows how to build a boat," he said. His smile dimmed. "I can't believe it's down underwater. I hoped to use that boat for many years to come."

Mac stuck his head in the door. He told Captain Pratt to wait where he was. While Pratt waited in the large interrogation room musing over the photographs, Brenda went to talk with Mac. He told her to give the presentation since she discovered the boat switch when Pratt took her to the harbor. Brenda happily agreed and was proud to know that Mac had such confidence in her. They discussed certain points to be made. While Brenda spoke, Mac would observe reactions from the small group of suspects.

"We know someone got into Wally's shop to get that engine back," Mac said. "It may have been Wally himself who did that, for all we know. As much as Bryce gets on my nerves, I can't see him jeopardizing his up-and-coming career by killing someone. Besides, he wouldn't have been so excited to race that boat if he knew it was ready to sink. Captain Scully remains a mystery."

"Maybe Captain Pratt knew the boats were switched. Maybe something happened the day he and Eddy went fishing." Brenda breathed deeply. "We'll find out before the end of this presentation. I'm going to lay out all the facts as we have them."

They heard the three men enter the front office area. Mac went out and took them to the designated room. He watched all three as their eyes landed on the photo display in surprise. Brenda followed them in and stood before them. Once they settled in their chairs, she began.

"Captain Pratt took these photos of his boat after Wally built it." She pointed to the photo showing the kitchen area. "As you can see, the curtains have sailboat designs in them. That was his preference and an important fact here. If you will note something else in the kitchen you will see that there is no clutter. It had only what he deemed necessary for a kitchen." She mentioned the salt and pepper shakers secured in a special holder so they wouldn't go flying when the boat took a sharp turn, a small skillet turned over on the stove and other incidentals needed in a kitchen.

"What does all of this have to do with anything?" Bryce asked in an incredulous tone. Brenda stared hard at him and he bent his head downward.

"If you will take a look at the engine Captain Pratt showed off so proudly to the other two captains you will see it is sparkling new. This engine was replaced by Wally since Pratt's original engine malfunctioned the week before on a fishing trip. The reality of the situation was that the engine could have caught the boat on fire, or it could have caused the boat to sink if the raw-water hose had ruptured. Am I right so far, Wally?"

"Yes, that is what I saw on the old engine. It looked as if someone may have purposely caused a rupture in the hose. I can't be sure of that but the engine itself was faulty and that's why it needed to be replaced."

"Where is the old engine, Wally?" Brenda asked. Mac was

scrutinizing everyone's faces carefully as they watched Brenda's presentation.

"I still have no idea. It's like I told you and Mac. I put it there and tagged it with the boat numbers and Captain Pratt's name on it. I wanted to take a closer look later when I had more time, maybe switch out a few parts. As you know, when you were in my shop earlier, the engine was nowhere to be found. I asked around and none of my guys had seen it, either."

"That's because we believe the engine was stolen from your shop and put back into the boat that sank. We believe the same person then killed Captain Eddy, though we don't know the motive." Brenda looked at Mac. "Perhaps you want to tell them our conclusion as to how Captain Eddy died."

Mac stepped forward. "When we saw the wooden barrel on the deck of the Eddy, we also noticed red marks down the outside of it. The marks were on one side and after examining Eddy's hands, it was determined he fought his killer, trying to pull his head from the water. The killer held his head under until he died. His upper clothing was wet and that told us it was unlikely that he could have drowned anywhere but in that barrel. It took a strong person to lift him and take him to his cabin where we found him." The men were quiet for a moment as they absorbed this information.

"I know a lot about boating," said Bryce, "but if the engine had been put back into the boat, why didn't it sink while sitting on the water, docked?"

"I'll ask Wally to answer that."

Wally explained why it would sink once the boat was running, if indeed the hose had been tampered with. Everyone seemed satisfied with his answer, though this scenario was no less shocking. Who would sabotage a boat like that? Brenda glanced at Captain Scully. His hands were large and his physique was muscular. This observation seemed more and more important, especially given Wally's known back injury; and though Bryce was fit, she doubted he could lift someone like Captain Eddy. Her eyes locked with Captain Scully's. He shifted several times in his chair.

"Whoever killed Captain Eddy had no idea that Detective Bryce Jones would be the one to take over the boat," Brenda continued, not looking away from Scully for an instant. "The person who put the old engine back in thought it would slow down the captain of that boat and cause him to lose the race. That person wanted Captain Eddy to lose, and in a big way. Unfortunately, the murderer decided that sabotage wasn't enough, and their intentions shifted to kill the captain of the boat, too."

Bryce watched Brenda with admiration. He thought she had not found her true calling. She was cut out for what she was doing at this moment. He watched her face raptly as she continued.

"You will now understand just why the kitchen and other areas of Pratt's boat are important to this crime. When I went onboard with Pratt last night to look at his boat for possible clues, it was the first time he had stepped on board since the race. And he was most surprised that the curtains in the boat were patterned with yachts instead of sailboats. Also, the counter was cluttered with small nautical knick-knacks. There were scuff marks on the floor that did not match any of his shoes." She looked at Pratt and smiled.

Mac stepped forward when Brenda looked his way. "The most notable thing of all in regard to this boat is that the name had been painted over. Someone painstakingly painted the name Pratt, but using a special light we were able to reveal that it originally had Eddy's name. In summary, gentlemen, the boats were switched." The silence in the room was palpable.

Captain Scully was the first to move in his chair. All eyes landed on him at the disturbance. He spread his hands on top of the table and took a deep breath.

"You don't have to look any farther," he said in a gravelly tone. "I was the one who switched the boats. It started as a joke at first. I was just going to show Eddy a thing or two about who's the best captain around here...until I heard him and Pratt talking about a recent fishing expedition. I usually went with them. We did everything together." His eyes pled with Captain Pratt. "We were like brothers, once. We did things together. But they had just left me behind."

"What about the engine?" Pratt asked, gobsmacked. "Are you the one who switched them?"

"Yes. It's easy enough for a strong man with a big truck. No one suspected a thing. I walked into your shop, Wally, early evening before the race day. Two of your workers were in the back out of sight. I suppose they were working on something late. The shop door was unlocked and I went in and found the original engine." He studied his calloused hands. "I did mean it to be a joke on Eddy. I expected Eddy to be slowed down out there on the water and lose the race. He was a good seaman and could take care of himself if anything happened."

Those in the room were stunned at his confession. No one said anything and all knew there was more to come. Scully finally looked at Brenda.

"I came into the coffee shop one morning, hoping to find Pratt and Eddy. While I ordered my coffee at the counter, I overheard them planning a fishing trip. They didn't see me because they were sitting way in the back of the shop in one of the secluded booths. Eddy appeared a quiet man to most, but he was excited during their conversation. He even suggested to Pratt they plan more things together out on the waters once the race was over." He bitterly turned to Pratt and spat out his next words. "Neither one of you mentioned me at all. Until that moment, I only thought about switching the engines as a joke. I was upset that after all these years my friendship meant nothing. Nothing."

Captain Pratt spoke first. "Good God, Scully, we didn't intentionally exclude you. If we had seen you come into the shop we would have called you over and asked if you wanted to join us. It was a spur of the moment thing. How could you do this?"

All eyes riveted again on Captain Scully. He seemed to have aged ten years from the time he started his story, sinking into his chair with despair.

"After I came up with the prank with the engines, I couldn't stop thinking about it. It made me sick at heart. It wasn't a joke anymore. I paid a local fisherman who is handy with painting boat names to paint over Eddy's name and copy Pratt's name there. I told him it was for a prank. He also helped me switch the places where the boats docked. I swore him to secrecy and he is truly innocent in everything that happened later. He had no idea of what followed once that part was done. I confronted Eddy about the planned trip. Wally had been speaking with all three of us down at the dock that night and then left. Pratt went back to Main Street. It was just me and Eddy. The night watchman was taking a break and I convinced Eddy to board his boat with me so we could talk more. He had no idea he was on Pratt's boat and not his...it was dark so he probably couldn't see too well." Scully coughed and then wiped his forehead with his hand.

He appeared reluctant to continue. "You've come this far, Captain Scully. You may as well finish it now." Mac's voice held command. "This is your chance to tell all of us what you did next."

Scully nodded, resigned. "I don't know what came over me. I was so mad, but Eddy argued the whole matter was an innocent one and that if I was bent on going with them I could go the next time. At that point, I had the feeling he didn't mean what he said. After all, everyone had heard how he bragged about how much fun he and Pratt had that day. They told jokes with each other and caught enough fish to take down to the market on the harbor. I asked him why they didn't call me up and take me along." He looked at Brenda again. "Fishing is my passion. I'd rather be doing that than out racing. And we've been like brothers for years. It burned me up, wondering why he didn't think of me. I had to ask him why. Why."

"What did Eddy say when you asked?" Brenda said.

"He said 'I guess I didn't think of you at all.' Can you imagine such a thing?" Scully seemed half broken as he said it, and Brenda almost had pity for the man, who hid this well of loneliness and despair beneath his outwardly jovial demeanor.

Mac thought Captain Scully was a little unhinged. Why would he get so upset over a simple fishing trip like that? It was as if he was a child on the playground left out of a game. No sooner had this thought crossed Mac's mind when Captain Pratt leaned forward toward Scully. "You're sounding like an immature school boy. This was one time we didn't go fishing together and you had to kill our friend over it? It just doesn't make sense to me."

Scully didn't answer at first. He finally spoke. "After being friends for thirty years you can't understand how hurtful it was to me. I love you both like brothers. We're more than family, out there on the ocean. I may have taken it too far. I have no excuse except to say the anger and disappointment I felt in the moment overtook me. I wasn't thinking rationally, I know, but the rage inside me caused me to strike out at Eddy in a way I'd never imagined could happen. He just made me so angry. I know I have a short fuse sometimes but that night..."

"What happened?" Mac asked.

"He said some harsh words to me in the cabin. We scuffled with one another until it seemed like I would burst, and my rage just took over. I would make him understand. I forced him to go up to the deck with me. I think he thought I did that so we could get some air and talk more reasonably. Instead I shoved him toward that barrel. I knew it was filled with water. I struck him again and... probably said some more things I shouldn't have...I remember I managed to get my arm around his neck to control him. He was surprised and that gave me an edge. I pushed him hard to the bucket and while holding him I shoved his face into the water. He fought like everything but by then I could barely see through my rage. I guess...I was determined to finish what I started. He finally took his last breath and was limp. I had to half carry him and half drag him to the cabin. He looked serene once I placed him on the bed. Then I realized how bad it would look and mopped up the marks made when I dragged him to the cabin. During the race, I knew the boat would sink, and take the rest of the evidence with it. But it was still terrifying when I saw young Bryce signal for help. When I turned around to reach his boat, I was prepared to stop the race officials from boarding it to inspect the engine, if need be. But that hose did all the work and the crime scene sank to the bottom of the harbor faster than I ever imagined. Now it's all gone. Everything." Scully stopped as if these last words had taken what was left of his spirit out of him. His voice was monotone and he barely moved.

Brenda was in shock at his confession. She realized this also meant that perhaps Scully had meant to pin the crime on Pratt, who was left with Eddy's original boat.

Mac quietly told Pratt, Wally and Bryce to wait in the lobby for him. He then called for two cops and told them to book Captain Scully for murder. Captain Scully simply sat at the table where he had been left alone, motionless.

Captain Pratt hung back and looked at his former friend. Only then did Scully stir.

"I regret my actions, Pratt. When Jones got ahead of us right away I had the feeling the boat was going to sink before the end of the race. Wally had mentioned it was a matter of a short time before it would have happened out on the water. I tampered with the hose to make sure it would sink. I didn't care that much about winning the race and I knew I had to help save Bryce when it happened. But I also wanted to give you the chance to win." He looked at his fellow captain with something akin to hope, as if this slim offering could possibly offset his monstrous crime.

Captain Pratt's eyes held sympathy mixed with disbelief and a hint of scorn for the man in front of him. In the end, his silence was its own reply. Captain Pratt did not reply to his former friend. He turned and joined the other two men in the lobby while Captain Scully was handcuffed and taken to his cell.

chapter ten

"It's been quite a day," Mac said to the other men in the lobby. "I want to ask the three of you to keep everything that was said in the interrogation room under your hats. There will be a trial and I'm sure the lawyers will be in touch for your testimonies as needed. But I trust the three of you to not let this terrible story spread around town. Please keep everything to yourselves."

The men agreed. Captain Pratt asked if he was free to leave Sweetfern Harbor. Mac told him he was free to leave but to let him know his whereabouts. He would be a witness at the trial and should expect to be called back soon. "You'll be asked details of your relationship with both Scully and Eddy. The jury will have to have enough to decide what happens to him." Wally and Pratt thanked the detective and left, still somewhat dazed. Bryce hung back to talk with Mac.

"You and Brenda did a good job, Mac. I can't figure out why you don't convince her to go to a Police Academy and make this a career for herself."

Mac laughed. "She has no interest in doing this full time, but I admit she is very meticulous in picking up clues and she knows just when to act on a hunch." They shook hands as friends and both were relieved to have cleared the air between them. Mac went back to his office when Bryce left the police station, and found Brenda in his office finishing up her notes. He smiled to see her there. She looked natural and right at home.

After the long, trying afternoon, the first glimmers of twilight were already descending over the town. "Let's get some fresh air, Brenda. A walk will do us both good."

She attempted a smile. "I know I initially thought Scully was the one, but now that we have heard his confession, his reasons still don't make sense to me at all."

"I suppose it was because he got out of control. Not a conscious decision. He admitted he has a short fuse but it still seems odd that he went so far. But we weren't there. I suppose we'll never know if there was something more to their fight than we were told."

Once outside, they breathed in the breezes that carried the scent of the sea air and walked in silence for a couple of blocks.

"I have not grown tired of the fresh air here. The ocean smells wonderful," Brenda said. "When I lived in Michigan I had no idea a place like this existed."

"I'm glad Randolph willed the bed and breakfast to you. If he hadn't, you would still be an assistant to that Private Investigator. Worse than that, I would never have met you." He pulled her to his side and kissed her on the cheek.

"My uncle was a very generous man," Brenda said. "I will always be thankful he thought of me in his will." Her forehead wrinkled. "It is hard to believe just a few days ago the three captains were jostling with one another over who would win the race. Now, one is dead and it happened at the hands of his friend who is now booked for murder. I would never have thought they would turn on each other to the point of taking a life."

"Jealousy is a strong emotion," Mac said. "I've experienced it myself since Bryce came back to Sweetfern Harbor. He's always been a flirt for as long as I've known him, but when he tries it with you, it's almost more than I can take. I can understand jealousy turning to anger."

"I can assure you Bryce has done nothing but harmlessly flirt with me. I can handle him and he knows it. I've gotten him to back off several times with ease. You have nothing to worry about along those lines, Mac. I know who I'm in love with." Her eyes teased him.

"That's a relief to me," he said. "You know, Bryce was dating a very nice woman for almost a year. Her name was Susan and she was a junior attorney for a large firm. I don't know what happened but they broke up. He pretends to be a player and a charmer, and he is, but I think he's hiding a good heart underneath. I thought they made a good pair but apparently something was going on that those on the outside didn't see." He paused. "I have a feeling he'll be leaving soon. I heard he's up for a big promotion in his department in Brooklyn."

By now they had walked from the station clear up the hill through town to the bed and breakfast, so they continued up to Sheffield House. Brenda sensed that Mac was reluctant to end their conversation even though it was time to say goodbye. She caught his eye. The teasing look was back.

"Where did you hide the ring I gave you?"

"I didn't want to wear it and have to answer questions about it if you weren't ready to make an announcement. It is hidden in a jewelry box in my apartment." Brenda kept her fingers crossed in her pocket, wondering if his sudden good mood meant what she hoped it did.

"Go and put it on. If anyone asks you about it, tell them. I'm ready to pronounce you my girl to the whole town. You are the woman I'm going to marry." The wide smile on her face pleased Mac and he grinned back at her. He waited while she ran upstairs to get the ring.

When she came downstairs, she handed him the sparkling jewel. "Let's start all over again. Act as if I never had this beautiful stone on my finger in the first place." Mac obliged and led her to the quiet library room in the back of the Sheffield. As they walked hand in hand, Brenda could feel her heart beating loudly in her chest.

In the twilight, the library had one single lamp glowing on a low table, and the polished wood of the bookcases gleamed in its light. Mac knelt down on the soft carpet on one knee and asked her to marry him. She said yes and he slipped the ring on her finger. Brenda had not been this happy since the first time he did it, but this time she knew it was more real, more solid, and more tested by time. His kiss on her lips warmed her entire mind and body.

When they pulled back from one another and were finally ready to exit the library together, Brenda made an observation.

"This place seems quieter than it should be. I wonder where everyone is." Her face clouded with confusion as she peeked into the hall. Even Allie was not at her post to greet guests who came in. She walked over to her office and glanced in. "I wonder where Allie could be. She should be here taking care of business." Brenda fidgeted a little bit, disappointed that she couldn't spill the good news right away.

Mac repressed a smile. "I'm sure they are all busy with important business, you can tell them soon enough. Come here, Brenda. I have something very important to say." She turned back to him. "I want to apologize for how I hurt you when I said we should keep the engagement quiet. Well, you are the light of my life and the woman I am going to marry, and you deserve a big announcement. You deserve that and so much more." His smile was tender as he held her in his arms. "So I have a surprise for you."

"What kind of surprise?" Brenda was a fan of surprises but his words puzzled her.

"You'll see." With that, he asked her to cover her eyes and he carefully led her through the house. She sensed they were walking toward the kitchen or the back porch, she wasn't quite sure. Then he leaned in close to her ear and whispered, "Okay, you can look now."

When Brenda opened her eyes, she was standing at the threshold of the door to the lawn, and she gaped. Lights were strung around the perimeter of the garden, twinkling in the darkness. Their light enclosed a large group of people from Sweetfern Harbor. Every staff member stood on the front edge of the crowd. Allie lit the last candle on a large cake on a table in the middle before joining her co-workers.

"Surprise!" they yelled. The crowd cheered and clapped as Brenda covered her mouth in amazement and blinked back happy tears. She hugged Mac and gazed out at the beautiful gathering. Together they stepped onto the lawn toward the cake that read 'Congratulations on your engagement Mac and Brenda' in fancy curly script with fondant roses around the edge. She recognized Hope Williams' handiwork immediately and felt encircled by the love of everyone in Sweetfern Harbor.

Phyllis hurried over to Brenda and gave her a big hug. "Congratulations Brenda, you are getting a good man. Now let me take a quick look at that diamond." Brenda held her hand out amid more bursts of joy that came from everyone who came up to embrace her and shake Mac's hand with happy wishes for the future couple.

"That's some stone, Mac," said Hope with a grin. "That must have set you back." She gave him a mock punch in the shoulder and laughed at her humor.

"I'd pay one hundred times that and more for the woman I love."

As soon as she got a chance, Brenda turned her face up to Mac. "I'm thrilled. I can't believe you thought of all of this. I love you, Mac Rivers." They kissed until someone shouted it was time to cut the cake and get the party going.

Music started to play from one of Brenda's favorite bands. Mac took her hand and led her to the dance floor set up under the trees. Everyone watched happily as they danced gazing into each other's eyes. Mac then waved his hand toward them all and invited them to join in on the dance floor. Soon it was filled with dancing couples. Brenda noticed Bryce when he stumbled a couple of times as he moved across the floor with Allie. She smiled to herself. Allie had hoped the handsome detective would one day take her in his arms and Brenda had to smile that the teenager's dream came true. She made a mental note to caution Allie later in regard to not taking flirty Bryce seriously. As for now, she reveled in the arms of the man she loved.

After a few dances, Jenny pulled her father and Brenda toward the table laden with a variety of food. Hope Williams, true to form, had brought not only the sumptuous cake but also decorated cupcakes to be placed at the end of the table. She told them congratulations again and hugged Brenda.

"I want to personally welcome you to our family, Brenda." Jenny's happiness was genuine. "I'm glad my father finally made it all public. You'll have to nudge him once in a while." She laughed and kissed her father's cheek. "You know how to choose a good woman, Dad." Brenda was happy to know that along with a husband came a daughter like Jenny.

They sat at a long table. Phyllis sat next to Brenda and the two women shared a look of deep excitement and joy at having each found the man they loved. "Phyllis, you must agree to be my Maid of Honor." The words caused a sudden tear to trickle down Phyllis' cheek. She nodded agreement since no words were possible due to the lump in her throat.

Brenda turned to the other women. Jenny sat next to her father. Allie and Molly were across from them with Hope and David Williams. Brenda pointed to each of the women one by one and said. "You will be my Bridesmaids." All of them, unlike Phyllis, found words. Allie made several enthusiastic suggestions about the wedding and Hope joined in. Brenda became aware that as long as she told them how she wanted it all to transpire, they would get it done.

"I don't know about a big fanfare like that," said Mac warily. Everyone shouted him down good naturedly and he put his arms around Brenda. "I'm defeated. I surrender!" Everyone laughed and told him he had no say in any of it. Jenny jabbed him on the arm and told him to just make sure he showed up the day of the wedding.

Brenda felt someone come up behind them and turned to face her fiancé's old friend.

"Congratulations to you both," said Bryce. "I'm really happy for you. Just know you'll have to keep Mac in line, Brenda."

Laughter spilled out again. "Sit down and eat with us," said Mac. He felt secure and comfortable with Bryce now that Brenda was his so publicly. Perhaps there was something to living life in the public eye, he reflected.

Bryce retrieved food and joined them. "I have some news of my own," he said. All eyes moved to him. "I'm going to stick around for quite a while. I've just been hired by Chief Ingram. He told me he needed a new detective since the town has been taking in more tourists than ever before." He looked around for responses.

"I think that's great," said David. "With everything going on around here I'm sure the police are stretched more than they used to be. We're not quite the tiny little village we used to be." He reached across the table and shook hands with Bryce.

Bryce turned to Mac. "I'll be moving back up to Sweetfern Harbor. Now I'll get to work with you all the time." Mac visibly rolled his eyes. Bryce winked at Brenda.

"I'm sure Mac will enjoy working with you," she said. Mac rolled his eyes again. She had a feeling they would be friendly competitors and, hopefully, spur each other to work better out of love and not spite.

"Maybe we will get a chance to do a night on the town one day after all, Brenda," Bryce said.

"Maybe as a double date, Bryce. But not with Allie," she teased. "She's not even eighteen yet. You really should find someone your own age and not rob the cradle." Bryce tried to defend himself as Allie blushed.

"Allie, you'd never be able to trust this one anyway, you're not missing out," Mac said playfully. "And, Bryce, you have to admit that Brenda's got you there. And don't get any ideas about my fiancé anyway. She belongs to me and me only."

Brenda changed the subject before the old jealousy returned. Nothing was going to spoil a night like this one. Several more friends from the town approached their table to offer congratulations to the happy couple. Then William Pendleton came up to shake Mac's hand, and his eyes landed on Phyllis with a smile. He turned back to Mac saying, "Sorry I'm late to the party, Mac. I am so happy to celebrate with you both."

"Where have you been all evening?" Phyllis asked him. "You missed the good news."

"I know all about the reasons for this celebration. I was caught longer than expected in New York City and just got back." He congratulated Brenda and Mac. Phyllis pulled up a chair next to her. He filled his plate and sat down.

As they chatted some more, Phyllis and William soon

appeared to be in their own world and everyone around them became secondary. They gazed adoringly at each other. Brenda leaned toward Mac and whispered, "Do you think we will still be so in love when we are that old?"

"I have no doubt at all about that."

"You're right. Our love will surpass all time."

Their eyes locked with notable passion. Suddenly, they were the only two people in the yard.

more from wendy

about wendy meadows

Wendy Meadows is a USA Today bestselling author whose stories showcase women sleuths. To date, she has published dozens of books, which include her popular Sweetfern Harbor series, Sweet Peach Bakery series, and Alaska Cozy series, to name a few. She lives in the "Granite State" with her husband, two sons, two mini pigs and a lovable Labradoodle.

Join Wendy's newsletter to stay up-to-date with new releases. As a subscriber, you'll also get BLACKVINE MANOR, the complete series, for FREE!

Join Wendy's Newsletter Here
wendymeadows.com/cozy

Made in United States
North Haven, CT
07 April 2024

51007436R00065